*To Gaby*

*Thank you for the read!*

# Close to Death

by

M. Antoine Louis-Jacques, M.D.

DORRANCE
PUBLISHING CO
EST. 1920
PITTSBURGH, PENNSYLVANIA 15238

Dorrance Publishing Co
585 Alpha Drive
Pittsburgh, PA 15238
Visit our website at *www.dorrancebookstore.com*

ISBN: 978-14809-37932
eISBN: 978-14809-37703

*To my parents, Charles and Saturna. To my children, Naisha Tonie and Marcel Alexandre, my lifelong inspirations.*

# Chapter 1

July 17, 2001
16:38

"Finally, it's quitting time," uttered Bill out loud to no one in particular.

By all accounts, this was just another great day in the life of Bill A. Presser, Chief of Anesthesiology at St. Mary Medical Center in Fresno, California. Bill had just dropped off Mrs. Koppel in the Post Anesthesia Care Unit, PACU, after her Hernia Repair Surgery.

However, he seemed distracted, totally disengaged as he relayed the post-op care orders to the nursing team that seem to always hang on to every word emanating from his mouth—he hated that. "But, in all fairness, those same kiss-ass nurses despised me too," he thought.

He finished his business and departed the PACU and managed a curt smile to all he encountered as he made his way down the hallway towards the Doctor's Lounge. Along the way, he passed Operating Rooms A and B that had their door shades up just enough for him to sneak a peek; he couldn't resist. There were giggles all around in Room A as the speakers blared something he barely recognized as decent music while Room B was vacant. He moved on.

He hesitated as he reached the door to the common lounge, thought better of bypassing it, and pushed it open at the last minute. He was pleasantly surprised that it was equally as empty as Room B. He entered and once inside, he scavenged through the fridge, found a Coke, and eyeballed it. It had a nametag taped to the side of the can. Bill tore it off with glee without so much of a glance at it and snapped open the top, not giving a damn as to whom it may have belonged to—finders' keepers, losers'...

Bill turned it over, drained its contents, and then slumped into the easy chair located in front of the TV that seemed to be perpetually tuned to the financial news channel. He was instantly irritated that the remote control was nowhere in sight.

In his search, Bill noticed the pile of incomplete charts that Medical Records left for him to peruse through for inconsistencies and missing signatures. For the life of him, he could not understand why they would not call ahead to see if he was even slightly interested in completing his delinquent charts on that day. Bill, once again, chose to ignore the heap even though he was fully aware that he could be suspended until such time that he completed them.

He soon let go of the trivialities of his daily grind and concentrated on the single most pressing issue currently in his life: money. He did four Laparoscopic Cholecystectomies, Gallbladder surgery, and two Hernia repairs all through private insurances. "Now that's easy money," he thought with a smile. "Another eighty-five hundred dollars towards community property," was the dour retort from the back of his head.

"Oh yeah! She earned every last penny while boozing herself at home didn't she? There's got to be a way to hide this money from Kelly and her bitch-ass lawyer—what's her name?"

"Trivial, trivial," he thought. "Soon enough, they will all be out of my life."

Bill slumped back into the chair after he finally located the remote control, wedged behind the sofa pillows, and switched the station to the Golf Channel. This was usually an exercise in futility, knowing full well that he could never sleep while watching a golf tournament; he usually finds himself fantasizing about being in contention on the back nine at Pebble Beach Resort. This time, he somehow managed to shut his brain off and relax just enough to drift off into a place he wished he could visit more often. He was a few tics away from slumber land when the silence in the room was interrupted by a loud shrill from the intercom, "CODE BLUE ROOM C."

As if once was not enough to paralyze him, the loudspeaker squawked again, "CODE BLUE ROOM C," and this time added, "Dr. Presser to Room C Stat."

Bill didn't immediately recognize the source of that sunken feeling in the pit of his stomach. Normally, he would relish the Adrenalin surge of an intra-operative resuscitation. 'A legal high,' he once called it. "This is as close to playing GOD as you'll ever get," was how a family member quoted him during a recent incident that was recounted in court. Apparently, he was more interested in the code than in actually saving the patient's life. He made no bones about it and although he won that suit, the judge summarily scolded him for his less than honorable professional conviction.

Bill summoned all his energy and sprung to his feet to scan the OR schedule of the day which was located immediately behind the sofa.

His worst fears were realized. Vicky, a Nurse Anesthetist and his on and off lover, was in Room C. He'd been avoiding her for weeks. How many ways can he tell her that he was not leaving his wife just for her and her alone? He must admit, she was persistent; she'd been relentless in her pursuit. She always returned for more punishment, despite the crude and ugly ways he'd been treating her of late. Ironically, that was the one character flaw that attracted Bill to this diminutive person. She was so unlike Kelly—his wife of eight years. Vicky was a go-getter. She was able to deflate Bill's ego with a glare and a simultaneous smile. She was one of the few people around here that was neither impressed nor intimidated by his gregarious persona, his titles, his awards, money, or his legendary attributes.

"Oh well, first things first," he thought as he rushed to her assistance. True to form and always at the most inopportune time, his cell phone went off, with the distinct ringtone from Kelly; he killed it without even looking at it.

"Gotta go rescue my peeps," he mused as he sauntered out of the room with enough pep in his step that he almost looked interested in saving this unfortunate soul coding on the OR table. They were already dead, for all he knew; the cavalry was seldom called in until they were well beyond the time that they could actually be of any help. Why should this time be any different?

His phone, strapped to his waist, rang again with Kelly's distinctive tone and he wanted to silence it but answered it as he continued his trek.

"Make it quick!" He snapped. "I'm heading to a code."

"Go ahead then," she nervously replied. "Nothing urgent except that I have great news to tell you. It'll keep 'till you get home. Love you!" And with that she hung up.

Bill shrugged at the silence. He hesitated and mumbled, "Love you? Wow! I haven't heard that in a long time. Oh well!" He said out loud and continued.

Vicky needed his help and that was enough motivation to ignore Kelly and hurry up and join the mayhem. His phone rang once more, this time in his generic ringtone. He ignored it while it rang and rang, until it went to voicemail.

There was already a small crowd of onlookers and helpers as Bill crashed through the double doors of OR C, making his usual grand entrance.

CPR was already in progress. Dr. Smith, the ER physician, was performing a cut down for intravenous access on the left leg, in the groin area. He was accessing the large femoral vein to be exact, which would give the resuscitative drugs a more direct route to the heart. There were a few physicians and nurses in the background observing the turmoil; just like vultures, basking in the sorrows of others. To his horror, Bill took notice of Vicky at the head of the table; she was obviously struggling to ventilate the lungs of the patient through a poorly fitting facemask. She grasped her chin and mask with both hands while the circulating nurse squeezed the bag in order to deliver oxygen to her lungs.

Judging by the loud, squeaky sound escaping from around the facemask, she could not possibly get enough oxygen to sustain her much longer.

'Dang!' he mused. To his bewilderment, he assessed that this resuscitation has indeed been going on far longer than before they called him.

The patient was a grotesquely obese female, blue to waist high from lack of proper oxygenation. "She's not likely to see another birthday," thought Bill as he deftly donned on a pair of latex gloves and a facemask.

The respiratory therapist busily aspirated, with a 10 cc syringe and a 22 gauge, 2 inch beveled needle, an ominously appearing dark, chocolate colored blood from the femoral artery in the right groin. Every textbook will tell you that you can't tell much from the color of blood. But, there was no mistaking that sample for completely de-oxygenated elixir. The implications were obvious. If he does not resuscitate this whale soon, she would be a goner.

A small team of nurses huddled about the crash cart, sorting out vials of emergency drugs; drugs that they have not seen since the last code blue some months or even years ago. The look on their faces surrendered the underlying fright within all in the room. They all knew how quickly a life could be lost in the operating room. Even in the best of hands, a patient without oxygen to the brain can die in less than three minutes. Fortunately or not, with the advent of newer and safer drugs and better hemodynamic monitoring, most but a few seasoned staff in the room had ever seen an intraoperative rescue, let alone an intraoperative death, but they all have heard of the horrific failures that have happened in the past.

At times like this, Bill would evoke the wisdom of his old mentor, Roger Von Phul, M.D., who passed away much too soon. Roger would always say, in his usual deep baritone voice, "Look around the room before you do anything, son. The fear you see in their eyes is not for the patient, it's for themselves. They know that if you fail, one of them would have to take over; we know, and they know, that they're as worthless as a penny with a hole in it. So, never let them see you sweat, son."

Over the years, Bill added his own version to the admonishments of his mentor. He had always made a point to catch the eye and wink at the prettiest Nurse in the room while enthralled in the heat of a resuscitation. This time was no different and that was not lost on Vicky either; this time however, a first in a long time, he winked at someone else.

"Note to self," she thought, "Fuck him!"

The anesthesia machine alarmed at a frantic pace. Chaos reign supreme in the room. Directions came simultaneously from all participants; it was a scene Bill thought was eerily similar to his days in Baghdad during the Gulf War.

Death warmed over the lifeless patient by the second. Bill could feel the presence of the ripper as he made his way to the cacophony of disorganized bodies in motion that made up a Code Blue Team.

"What happened?" He asked as he placed a hand on Vicky's left shoulder as he approached the table. He wondered if he would get to be a hero and save the day or would this blubberous mass prematurely meet her maker.

Vicky took a deep breath in response to his touch. In a trembling voice, she replied, "I can't get the airway. I think she's gonna need a cricothyroidotomy," she added in a hurried tone.

"Like hell she does!" He exclaimed more forcefully than he intended.

A cric—for short, is a small incision made at the level of the Adam's Apple where a breathing tube can be introduced into the lungs when one cannot be had in the old fashion way, through the mouth or nose.

To Bill however, it was an utter sign of failure. He had yet to meet an airway he couldn't intubate. At least, not until the next one; he always tried to humbly tell himself.

"What on God's earth is going on here? Get all of these goddamn people out of here!" He snarled.

"Listen up!" He proclaimed loudly. "If you don't have any skills to contribute here then get the hell out of this room, now!"

The room went eerily silent, save for the machinery of surgery; everyone took notice, but no one left. He leered at a few of the underlings who fled, if for no other reason but to escape his poignant glare. Otherwise, no one moved. Visibly perturbed, he turned his attention back to Vicky. Once upon a time, his voice would have commanded all in this hospital.

"What the hell was this world coming to?" He thought.

"Who the hell is she? Get all of these damn people out of here for crying out loud," he said again. This time, he was staring directly at Donna, the charge nurse. "This is not a goddamn circus!" He shouted.

"She's Nikki Ryan. She's having her gallbladder removed," whispered Sheila, the scrub tech, in his ears.

"Well, that seems appropriate," He replied out loud. "The five 'F's' of Gallbladder disease," he mused, "Fat, Female, Fertile and Fucking Forty."

"A few push-aways from the dinner table could have avoided this scene," he added.

The name didn't mean much to him until he realized that the face behind the mask, performing CPR was none other than the infamous Dr. Bertram Ryan, Chief of Pathology, her husband of twenty plus years. He was too scared to be perturbed by or respond to Bill's remarks.

For once in his life, Bill wished he'd shown better discretion. He was never known for his tactfulness. On more than one occasions, he was reprimanded for his crude and boorish behavior towards the nursing staff.

"Too late now," he mumbled. "Move over, let me try." With one motion, he shoved Vicky out of the way; she practically fell off the sitting stool. Bill quickly replaced her at the head of the table. Without realizing it, Vicky instinctively reached for her equalizer, a syringe full of Succinylcholine, a paralytic agent, located behind her on the anesthesia cart. She felt for the ten cc syringe like a menacing scepter and fantasized about emptying it into his gluteal muscle. He would stop breathing and be dead in less than three minutes. "What a fucking asshole he can be at times," she thought.

"Get me a MAC 4 blade," he shouted. "I need better visualization of the vocal cords. Suction! HURRY!" Instructions from Bill came at a frantic pace.

With unmistakably skilled precision, Dr. Presser attempted to secure the airway. The whole room grew quiet again, knowing that this was the 'make it or lose it' moment that they'd all read about in their respective textbooks. No one truly wanted to admit that they were pulling for the ripper but deep down they were fascinated with the scene, wishing they could experience a once in a lifetime event at the expense of no one else but the infallible Dr. Presser. Bill took in a deep breath and went through the process of adjusting the table to chest level. He took inventory of the instruments and the assorted pre-filled syringes located immediately behind him on the anesthesia cart, the various monitors and of course, his audience in front of him. Again, Bill took time out to locate and smile at the pretty nurse from earlier. If she was duly impressed, she just might have become his next concubine by night's end.

With his left hand, his fore fingers to be exact, he pried open her mouth and immediately, a gush of foul smelling secretion—bile, greenish brown in color—welled out of the mouth.

Instinctively, he turned her head all the way to the right and allowed the contents to drain out of her mouth. He instantly regretted that move as the copious contents spilled over the side of the narrow OR table and onto his shoes. And of course, they once again were worn without any shoe covers. How many times has Kelly reprimanded him for ruining yet another pair of expensive shoes? "Who the hell pays for them anyway," he thought.

"Where my mind wanders..." he thought as he shook his head visibly enough for a few in attendance to notice and wonder if their odds of a bad outcome had just improved. Their pulses quickened with excitement and Bill took notice and grinned in turn. Even through his shielded face, he felt that they should have appreciated his comfort level. Surely they must know that the Master was fully engaged and in charge. Game on!

He reached for the suction hose, but nothing was attached to it. He rolled his eyes at Vicky, and she quickly reached in the anesthesia drawer and pulled out a Yankauer tip and attached it to the suction tubing. He tested it against his hand; it was feeble.

"I need more power on this damn suction." He yelled as he gaped open the mouth once again; the lava flow had abated. A small team of OR techs scrambled to fix the suction bucket as he continued through the progression of setting up to secure the airway; it was her only chance of surviving this episode.

He encountered more secretions. "The bane of my existence," he thought. It was truly the sole reason why he should hate Anesthesia. You come in contact with some God-awful smelling shit while intubating a patient. NPO after midnight means just that, Nil Per Os, nothing by mouth, after midnight. I guess some folks do not consider semen, alcohol, and other such items as food. People always think they can fool their Anesthesiologist by sneaking a little sip overnight or a small piece of candy to 'freshen up.' The reality of it is that it is not what you put in your mouth that we are concerned about, rather it is the physiologic response to it. The stomach creates large amounts of acid in preparation for digestion. The stomach lining is well protected, but the lungs are not. Throw up during surgery and aspirate it, and it's kaput for you.

"She probably did inhale some of that crap," he thought—mortality as high as 70% is associated with aspiration of this kind. "We'll worry about that later," he said to himself and with that, he gripped the laryngoscope in his right hand, which always confused most hardy OR personnel as the standard grip is with the left hand. However, after his 3 surgeries, Bill had never regained enough strength in his left elbow to perform a true laryngoscopy in an emergency situation using his left hand. He had to have reversed blades made especially for him, the opposite of the standard equipment; they were not too different than a right- versus left-handed set of golf clubs was how he would explain it every time that conversation arose.

He inserted the scope through the gaping mouth and gently swept the tongue from left to right, again the reverse of normal, while applying gentle and continuous upward pressure with the laryngoscope. He avoided rocking the blade forward or backward on the upper and lower incisors. He struggled to see the vocal cords, located in the back of the throat just behind the Epiglottis, amidst the bounteous amount of vomitus and the swelling caused by Vicky's earlier attempts at securing the airway.

"WOW!" He exclaimed to himself. It has been 15 long years since he craved to be somewhere else other than the theater of a live resuscitation. "Where else can you play GOD, be a hero, get the chick, and not get blamed if the fucker dies?" He remembered his Chief Resident telling him this whenever the frantic call of 'CODE BLUE' would chime over the loud speakers at Saint Somefuckingwhereelse Hospital, as he likes to call the 'U' Hospital in San Diego.

For the first time in a long while, Bill could sense perspiration beading up on his forehead. He was genuinely scared.

"Cricoid, I need more Cricoid pressure," he yelled as he repositioned the hand of the nervous, yet eager medical student on the throat, just above the Adam's Apple. Properly applied Cricoid pressure serves dual purposes. It can provide posterior displacement of the vocal cords towards the back of the throat, thus enabling Bill direct visualization of where to place the endotracheal tube and it can also seal off the esophagus and prevent any more of the stomach contents from welling up and ending up in the lungs. The only bad place for the tube to end up would be down the esophagus, negating all the above processes, not a good choice. Bill had been the recipient of such an ill placed breathing tube and was sprayed with regurgitant all over his face under high pressure from patients who'd vomited through that tube. His Mentor, Dr. Von Phul would always say, "Son, the only thing worse than placing the tube in the esophagus is leaving it in the esophagus. If you recognize it right away, no harm no foul; just take it out and relocate it in the trachea." He would add to that, "Shit happens all the time. The only thing that keeps it off your brand new shoes is how quickly you can wipe your ass, son." 'Always be ready to wipe your ass,' was the take away Bill had as his mantra from that day on.

It was amazing how calm and collected he appeared on the outside to all in attendance, while a fierce storm raged inside. Only Vicky, however, knew of the real battle that raged within him; she wished she could tell all but thought better of it and decided to let it ride.

Sometimes, she resented him for being so perfect all of the fucking time. With all of this commotion, the thought reoccurred to her. She reached and uncapped the syringe of Succinylcholine. She knew she could discharge it into his ass and no one would even notice. He would writhe in agony, stop breathing, and be dead in less than three minutes. No one would suspect a thing short of the stress of the resuscitation on his tired and worn out old heart.

Her whole demeanor softened. She regretted the thought and cleared it from her heart as quickly as it surfaced, knowing full well that she didn't mean a word of it.

"Oh! How I have tried to hate this man on so many occasions," she thought.

"His charm always cut right through me."

Vicky's trek through wonderland was quickly interrupted by a loud shriek from the cardiac monitor.

"She's gone flat line!" Stated a voice from the back of the room. "Her O2 Sat is dropping fast. We're loosing her!"

The intensity and noise level in the room foretold of what was to come. Undaunted and unflappable, or so it seemed, Dr. Presser forged on. Every hair on his body stood at attention. His jaw clenched; sweat freely ran down his forehead and his anal sphincter was in spasm.

An overzealous Medical Student promptly delivered a sharp thump to the patient's chest, followed by chest compressions, just as he remembered reading from his outdated American Heart Association's manual on resuscitation.

Dammit! The laryngoscope was jarred out of the patient's mouth and clanged loudly on the floor and disappeared under the OR table. In what he can best describe as a reflexive move, Dr. Presser instinctively reached and grabbed this poor student by his scrub shirt and yanked him towards him for a much-deserved facial.

"You're happy?" He yelled into his face. "I couldn't see a fucking thing with all of those damn compressions. Did I tell you to beat on her chest?"

"No!"

"So you want to be a fucking Cowboy and save the day is that it? I'll tell you when to resume CPR son. It's on you if she dies!"

If looks could only kill...Bill finally let go of him and the poor student retreated to the back of the room. When all eyes finally left him and returned to Nikki, he quietly slipped out of the room for a good cry.

In a surreal and slow motion scene, Bill grabbed and put together another set of scope and blade and resumed his effort at securing the airway. All that can be heard was the thunderous roars of the machinery of surgery as he restarted the process with the laryngoscope.

All of the monitors alarmed simultaneously. The EKG monitor emitted a continuous tone signaling the absence of a heartbeat. The Pulse Oxymeter, which measures how well the blood is saturated with Oxygen, buzzed erratically. The tone, with good oxygenation is usually a high-pitched beep synchronized to the heartbeat. Now, it is an ominous low constant tone signaling the absence of a heartbeat and a lack of adequate oxygenation. The $CO_2$ monitor registered very little Carbon Dioxide—foretelling of the lack of circulation and proper ventilation by the lungs. Taken all together, there was no mistaking the absence of a beating heart and thus, a lack of proper oxygenation to the brain; by now the death clock was down to two minutes and counting.

The ever-changing chimes told the story. The grim reaper was amongst us; it was only a matter of time before Mrs. Ryan would transition to the afterlife.

With further manipulation of the laryngoscope, Bill was able to locate the Epiglottis in the back of the throat. "No wonder Vicky was having difficulties visualizing the vocal cords," he thought to himself. "She's got a false passage." The anatomy was so distorted from the trauma caused by multiple attempts at securing the airway with the firm metallic laryngoscope and blade that he was having a hell of a time himself discerning the usual landmarks.

"I can see why this was a bitch to secure." Despite several attempts at repositioning her head, he was still unable to visualize the vocal cords that were well bunkered behind the Epiglottis,

"I've got one and only one chance to do this," he thought. Four point three seconds left on the clock.... down by a point.

"Give me the damn ball!" He said out loud to no one in particular, followed by his usual humming that was always apparent to all in attendance except him.

It was amazing where his mind predictably wandered to at times like this.

Bill blindly reached behind him on the cart for more Succinylcholine. This would help to relax the neck and jaw muscle and allow for better visualization of the back of the throat.

"Ouch! Shit, I fucking stuck myself," yelled Bill as he felt the full effect as an inch and a half, eighteen-gauge, beveled needle spear his left index finger. Vicky almost fainted as she realized that she had left a used, bloodied, and uncapped needle on top of the cart; it was a no-no in this day and age of universal precaution against contagious diseases.

Bill scoffed at her as he grabbed the correct syringe and injected 8 cc's into the IV line and squeezed the Saline bag to hasten the medicine into the patient. As he waited for the medicine to take effect, Bill attempted to suck on his finger to stop the oozing but he forgot that his face was veiled and jammed his finger into the mask. He groaned out loud at his faux pas and returned his full attention to the patient.

Bill took a long deep breath and after ten long seconds, Bill re-attempted to intubate the patient.

To his pleasant surprise, he noted better relaxation and mobilization of the neck muscles and felt optimistic at his chance of success.

Suddenly, the vocal cords emerged from beneath the Epiglottis. Bill cringed at the thought of being this close and not being able to finish the task at hand. It had been a while since he lost a patient, which was a thought he quickly buried deep within the recesses of his mind.

"No green shit, regurgitants on the chords," he murmured to himself. "She's lucky. She probably did not aspirate after all. If any O2 went to the brain during CPR and we're able to restart her heart, she might make it after all. She may no longer be a concert pianist but at least she'll be able to recognize the freaking piano." He was always fond of that saying during times like this.

With deft precision, Bill slipped a 7.0 endotracheal tube into the back of her throat. The best orgasm, he thought, as his anal sphincter relaxed with the unmistaken sensation of the ET tube sliding past the vocal chords and sliding over the ridges of the trachea.

"Resume chest compression!" He barked out to no one in particular. "It's a good thing that I have this mask on. I couldn't let my public in on just how nervous and yet relieved I was," he thought.

With that thought, he inflated the pilot balloon on the tube, which helped to keep it secured in place and just as important, effectively seal the trachea from any more aspiration into the lungs. Bill then taped the tube to her cheeks, securing it in place. He then connected it to the anesthesia machine and proceeded to manually squeeze the bag and ventilate the lungs with 100% Oxygen.

Bill grinned as he marveled at the signs of a successful intubation: the mist of moist, warm air in the tube with expiration, bilateral chest expansion, a smooth, albeit elevated $CO_2$ tracing, and an ever improving Oxygen saturation on the monitors. The gradual transition from a dusky gray color to a healthy pink, almost normal hue was the final confirmation that she was being oxygenated. For all of her troubles, her lungs sounded pretty clear on auscultation. Suddenly, Bill emerged from the slow motion of his reverie and into the double time of a live resuscitation. This was still all artificial as the chest compressions continued.

"What's her rhythm?" He asked.

"V-Fib Now!" Was the immediate retort from someone in the crowd. "Continue CPR."

"Epinephrine, 1 amp STAT" was ordered and given.

"Charge the paddles!"

"Synchronized counter shock!"

A loud 'thud' was heard as the machine discharge 250 joules of thundering electrical power into the patient. Her body almost levitated off the table with the severe muscular contractions that ensued from the electrical jolt, contracting every muscle fiber that was still connected to the grid.

A plume of smoke emanated from her chest where the pads contacted her skin.

"No Response."

"Recharge at 300!"

Again, 'thud'—as the body shook even more violently from the higher electrical charge. Another fine plume of smoke rose from the burn marks left on the chest from the same defibrillator pads. The smell will leave you with an indelible perspective of rare steak at dinnertime.

All quieted, as all eyes fixated on the cardiac monitor. Once all the artifacts from the electrical activities dissipated, all that remained was beautiful sinus rhythm with a few premature ventricular beats.

"All Right! We got her back," said someone in the back of the room. The look and sound of relief was well evident in all.

"Lidocaine, 2mg per Kg followed by a drip at 1mcgm/kg/min STAT!"

Within a few minutes, calm and a sense of order was restored in the room. The patient's vital signs stabilized. On face value, there were no apparent sequellae from the preceding events; at least none that can be discerned until she actually wakes up, if she ever does.

The nurses and techs began to mill about, undoing the mess of a resuscitation. No one wanted a reminder of what just occurred. There were numerous vials, bottles, IV bags, syringes, and needles strewn about the room. They went about cleaning up while someone attempted to restore some dignity to Nikki Ryan by covering her up with a warm blanket. The nakedness of a resuscitation is never noticed until the very end. All eyes averted the patient as if suddenly aware of her humanity.

"Can we prep and get on with this operation?" asked the surgeon, Dr. Williams, who was standing just outside the room during the cardiac arrest.

He probably snuck out in time to check and make sure that his malpractice policy was up to date.

"Hell no!" was the joint response from Vicky and Bill. Gallbladder surgery is an elective procedure. There is no need to subject the patient to further anesthetic and surgical risk in the face of the events of the day. For all we know, she was already so 'gorked' out from her ordeals that surgery would be useless. The better part of valor is to call it a day, transfer her to the ICU, assess the damage, if any, and allow her to recover and come back on another day if surgery is still deemed necessary.

The color had finally returned to Dr. Ryan's face. He nervously slipped off his mask and managed a smile as he fumbled to remove his gloves and thank Bill, with a firm two-handed handshake, for his heroics. This is truly the only area that makes Bill uncomfortable. He relishes the limelight. However, he is unable to accept all the adulations that come with the territory.

The crowd started to dissipate as fast as it had gathered. Some of the nurses were busy cleaning up the mess that was made while someone wheeled the crash cart out of the room; a good sign to all the onlookers outside the room.

"You know that you will need to be tested on account of the needle stick," managed Dr. Ryan with a feeble voice.

Bill knew it was pointless to argue but his face betrayed his frustration. State regulation dictates that when anyone is stuck with a potentially contaminated needle, both parties must be tested and followed for contagious or infectious diseases.

"Stop by the lab, I'll have one of the techs draw the blood from you. We already have a sample from Nikki, and I can vouch for her," said Dr. Ryan as he forced a smile. "I'll send you the results as soon as they are available." Bill quietly dismissed Dr. Ryan and the rest of the OR crew as he attempted to slip out of the room.

"By the way," Dr. Ryan added, "I'll need an audience with you soon, Dr. Presser. We need to go over some great ideas I have for the Wellbeing Committee and the Senior Circle Foundation before the next meeting tomorrow."

"Weird," Bill thought, "for a guy who almost lost his wife five minutes ago to be fixated on trivial committees. Weird dude," Bill thought again and walked out of the room.

"Not so fast Bill," came the voice from behind him, as he stepped into the corridor.

There was no need to turn around. Vicki's voice always scored right through him like the cold steel of a razor sharp surgical knife.

"I couldn't let you get away without so much as a thank you. You saved her life—mine too for that matter." She nervously snickered.

"Enough already," he thought. "That's part of my job." He sheepishly replied.

"You needed help. I would have done it for anybody. Besides, we both know that it was sheer luck that I got the tube in."

"Gee! Thanks! For a moment there, I was feeling special Bill. I thought you were concerned about my wellbeing. Silly me!" She exclaimed as she approached him. His indifferent gaze stopped her advance.

"Will I see you later? Call me please. I really want to see you Bill."

"Oh! I can't. I almost forgot. Kelly called me two or three times before the code. I've got to get home. Get this," he added, "she's fixing dinner tonight. She supposedly has great news to tell me when I get home."

That stung Vicky and her face showed it.

"I've asked you not to talk to me about that woman Bill. You know how I feel about you Bill—you belong with me. I can make you so much happier—you know that."

"Not here Vicky, please. I'll call you ok! I promise—soon," uttered Bill, as he hurriedly turned on his heels and disappeared down the hallway, into the dressing room.

"Let me out of here before Old Man Murphy strikes again." In no time, Bill was dressed and headed out toward the parking lot. Half way down on the elevator, he realized that he had conveniently bypassed the lab.

Reluctantly, when the elevator reached the ground floor, Bill returned to the third floor and for once in his life, he decided to do the right thing.

Three sets of slow yet deliberate knocks on the door went unanswered. Bill was visibly steamed that no one was in the lab. Just as he was about to put his fist through the glass doors, he caught sight of shadowy figures emerging from the back of the room. Gail, a new hire in the lab, opened the door as she finished adjusting her coif and clothes. Bill noticed that Dr. Ryan, who was equally disheveled, quickly reached and closed his office door, which was in the same direction that Gail emerged from. She apologetically let him in and quickly ushered him to a bench. Much to her surprise, and his, she drew two complete red and purple top vials of blood from Bill without much resistance trauma or comments. As she finished, Dr. Ryan, now neatly attired, emerged from his office.

He exchanged small pleasantries with Bill, thanked him again for earlier, and promised to personally complete the tests and have them available by the next morning. The worst was over. Bill didn't have to let on how truly he despised being at the sharp, receiving end of a needle-again. He gathered his belongings and quickly headed out the door, down the hallway into the elevator for the parking lot. "Let's try this again," he said.

# Chapter 2

Bill was finally out of the hospital and went into the short covered portico toward the parking lot. Rain! It was not just rain, but fucking buckets of it. With the amount of it already on the ground and the anger in the current precipitation, there did not seem to be an apparent end in sight.

"This is supposed to be a desert for crying out fucking loud." That was one of the appealing virtues as to why he relocated here from the Northwest. It was dark, but dry when he came in early this morning; Bill didn't recall this on the forecast from last night's newscast.

"I just washed the dammed car yesterday," he thought, "and now I have to remember where I put that rain-check ticket from the carwash." He could immediately hear Kelly. "I always fucking hear Kelly-talking to me—no, yelling at me, that this wouldn't have been an issue if I had used the car wash service that she recommended. Not only do they come to the house, you wouldn't have to keep track of any silly little ticket. But nooooo! It was way too expensive, says the guy who doesn't think twice about a stupid country club membership that costs in the high five figures." For a couple that managed very little conversation when in close proximity to each other, she apparently could fill his head with bullshit and a running diatribe all day long.

Bill was fully aware that she only popped up in his head lately when he was either upset or reminiscing about old times, which had been occurring quite frequently of late, but never about real time events.

Once upon a time, the mention of her name would have Bill radiate a luminous aura about him that could be seen from miles away. Now, he needed to be three Martinis down to even recall the good times. Once there, he could spend countless minutes or hours in that place which would inevitably culminate in sheer hatred of her once he arrived at that familiar conclusion as to why his world was upside down. "It's all her fault," he steamed.

"Christ!" He yelled as he stepped into a water puddle; another wasted pair of Ferragamo's. "What else is gonna go wrong today?" He smirked as he realized that he shouldn't have asked that question but he'd seen enough for one day.

Bill via a circuitous route, located his car on the lower level parking lot. He got in, settled in, and stayed awhile as he tried to regain his composure. Several deep breaths later, life was again manageable. He reached and unloaded the CD magazine, finding its contents acceptable, he then shuffled them and reloaded the magazine into the dashboard. He punched in his selection, leaned back, closed his eyes, and enjoyed the music. Calming his nerves, he pulled out of the lot and on to Main Street after what seemed like hours in the parking lot. Traffic was already backed up. This translated into a forty-five minute ride home to Clovis Terrace.

As much as he cherished his time alone, Bill was fully aware of the tendency for his mind to drift far away from the unpredictable traffic of the 180 and the 168 Freeway when he was in his solitude. He would simply loose himself in thought and pay very little attention to the ever changing cacophony of cars whizzing by him, and sometimes worse, not moving at all. On several occasions, he found himself several exits beyond his, wondering how the hell he got there.

To that end, his absent-mindedness had also accounted for numerous close calls and several rear-ended accidents on the freeway over the past few years. Kelly, ever worried about his driving, had urged him to see a doctor about his memory lapses; he of course, refused. How could he explain to her that he would rather be lost in his thoughts than live in the real world with her? She also urged him on numerous occasions to consider getting a driver; Lord knows they can afford it. As outrageous as seeing a doctor was, a driver was an even more moronic idea to think that he could give up control of his comings and goings to some yahoo that he didn't even know. "Another Bozo in my house! Yeah right."

"Great!" He added. "If I didn't know better, I'd swear that Kelly enjoyed needling me knowing full well how much I hate strangers in my business, my shit! I've told her that on so many occasions!" Bill thought.

Bill lumbered his brand new Vanquish down the road and to his surprise, made it on to the 180 on-ramp in no time. "What a magnificent piece of machinery," he thought as he accelerated and merged into traffic heading away from the Big City lights towards Suburbia America. "Maybe I'll be home sooner than I thought. Joy! Great joy," he muttered out loud as he realized the irony of his thoughts.

The sky was aglow with a lightning show and now, a fine mist was blowing in a northerly direction. For some reason, unbeknownst to him exactly why, those sights took him back to freshman year in college—more precisely, Physics 101. "There should be a loud crash after each flash," he thought, "or is it the other way around?"

He smirked lightly as he realized that the sounds were muffled by the fantastic insulation in the car; hence, no noisy thunder after each flash.

"No American made car could do this," he thought out loud. Every now and then Bill found the need to defend his own vainness. "I've worked hard for this shit," he uttered out loud. "I deserve every bit of what I've got," as if someone not quite visible in the car needed justification.

Once again, Bill slowly drifted into his own little world, his own private time to spend with his favorite person—himself.

Even in his own selfish world, Bill was easily reminded of the long and arduous road to his success.

At the age of six, Bill relocated with his parents and only sister to the island of Haiti. Charles Presser, a Pentecostal Missionary Minister and his father, submerged himself in the plight of the Haitians and jumped at the chance to join a crumpling and dilapidated church on the outskirts of Port-au-Prince. The truth is that no one else but Charles volunteered for that mission.

What started out as a fairy tale, a true 'Robinson Crusso-esque' trip quickly faded when they arrived on site. In a sweltering 95-degree and 90% humidity day, they boarded a 'Tap-Tap' taxi, from the airport, loaded with at least 20 or more people over its capacity of eight, for the long trip to the church. The ride was a stark contrast between the picturesque mountains and lush hills of Petion-Ville and the shear terror and imminent probability of plunging down the rugged cliffs into an abysmal ravine at each and every turn.

Despite his dad's reassurance, Bill recalled the many harrowed close calls and the multiple turns made on three wheels with the fourth perilously hanging over the embankment. It must be the norm he thought, as his family seemed to be the only ones perturbed by the ride.

The Island had a unique smell, he recalled, a pungent yet aromatic essence that permeated throughout the country. He remembered the many shades of green he encountered, from the lizards, the frogs, and parrots flying from tree-top to treetop, to the lush vegetation, unrecognizable from his library books. Through today, there are certain fragrances that could immediately transport him back to those tranquil and innocent days in Port-au-Prince.

Bill often recollected the many long trips to the water spigot with a bucket as big, if not heavier, than his skinny frame. Back then, it felt like a mile away. But on a return trip some years later, it took him a while to locate this water-spout that was actually less than fifty steps away from the house. Nonetheless, that was still a world farther away than the crybabies of today, complaining at every turn on how rough they had it.

Bill did not see running tap water and indoor plumbing again until the age of fifteen. It was a small wonder he survived his earlier childhood; it was ravaged with diseases and political unrest, coup d'états and so on. In his naiveté, Bill recalled an incident in which a plane—he was always fascinated with planes—seemingly struck several birds as it flew along the countryside. He would observe the contact and the birds subsequently falling out of the sky.

Feeling quite repulsed by the senseless attack on these defenseless animals, he paid little attention to the loud noise and the ball of fire that followed. It wasn't until years later, ever the historian, which he read of the failed attack on the capital, which happened to coincide with his simplistic memory of that day. As archaic and embattled his early life was, Bill sometimes clamored for its simplicity; no time clock to punch, no weather forecast or stock market ticker to stay ahead of. And for that matter, he chuckled, no fucking divorce attorneys.

His serenity was quickly interrupted by the sound of his pager echoing in the car.

"Who the hell could this be?" Twenty million possibilities flashed through his head. "Shit!" He uttered, "I forgot about Kelly," as the house number scrolled across the LED screen of his pager.

He put the pager down on the center console and reached in his coat pocket, located on the hook behind his seat, and fumbled for his cell phone. He finally located it while trying to remain within the boundaries of his lane; no small feat as he came close on several occasions to an untimely encounter with the car in the adjacent lane to his right.

He composed himself until he felt that he could control his sarcasm and punched in the house number on the phone, speed dial #2.

Ring…Ring… Bill grew a little perturbed as time passed without an answer. He could never figure out why anyone (Kelly) would page him and take so long to answer the damn phone when he was courteous enough to call right back. It was so inconsiderate of his precious and limited time. If he could habitually call back immediately, the least they could do was to pick up just as swiftly.

"Hi Honey, where are you?"

"About thirty minutes away," was the monotonous reply, laced with all the sarcasm he could muster.

"Great! Dinner should be ready by then. I have such wonderful news; I'm so excited." He could hear and sense the emotion in her voice. "No!" she said. "You're going to have to wait until after, after-dinner. See you soon," and the line abruptly went dead. Again!

In shock, Bill stared into the phone. He couldn't believe that she actually hung up on him, twice in one day. What'd gotten into her lately? What could possibly put her in such a gleeful mood? She must have discovered another loophole entitling her to all of my assets for life. Bill was visibly disturbed by his not too funny thoughts. Even though they decided to call off the divorce proceedings, Bill couldn't help but wonder what else she had up her sleeve.

He turned up the stereo—deep bass, clear trebles and silky smooth vocals. Just the way he liked it as Nina Simone, 'The Folks Who Live on the Hill' loudly filled the car.

In no time, he was back into his reverie state, oblivious to his surroundings.

However, he did realize that it was imperative that he continued to act as if he was actually interested and committed to being at home. He must admit, she has made a concerted effort at being a better housemate of late. If only she had heeded his requests and demands early on in the marriage to stop the naggings and suspicions about his shenanigans at the hospital. So what if she was right more often than not? It was still her overactive imagination rather than any overt proof of his wrongdoings that fueled her antics. It seemed so simple to Bill that she was the one who drove him away from home. Besides, turnabout was fair play, wasn't it?

He frowned.

Things were never quite right enough for her. It didn't take long for him to realize that his only reprieve was to stay away altogether. He used to justify that they couldn't actually fight if they were never in the same place.

"How did things get this bad?" He wondered. "Once upon a time, she was the love of my life—no less at first sight," he added.

He had grown accustomed to ignoring her so much that he couldn't remember the last time he longed for her the way he used to when they first met.

Bill once again slipped back into his quiet place, displacing all thoughts of Kelly; so much so, he almost missed his exit—again. At the last minute he careened off the ramp, missing a VW Rabbit by a hair. Both drivers exchanged the usual expletives and gestures and went about their merry ways.

Bill regained his composure as he saw a car being pulled over by a police cruiser ahead of him on Fryant Road. It was a reminder on the crackdown on speeding and drunk driving going on citywide.

It all started when the daughter of a prominent local politician was mowed over by a drunk, illegal driver a while back. Apparently, it was his third offense. The irony was seemingly lost on all, save for Bill, that it was the politicians that lobbied for leaner sentences and community services for what they called a rehabitable offence. It was their answer to the overcrowding of the local jails, rather than building new ones out in the desert somewhere, anywhere far away from civilization.

Never mind if the bastard was deported on the first offense, this whole dialogue would be moot.

Bill instinctively set his cruise control to 45mph and continued all the way home without further distractions. Shortly after, Bill pulled into his side driveway and disappeared into the garage, closed the door, and remained behind the steering wheel with the car idling for quite some time. Enough time had passed for Kelly, who had heard the garage door open and close, to be concerned and check up on him.

As she suspected, he was fast asleep at the wheel. She stayed at the door and stared at him, reminiscing of days of yore. He has grown into such a restless sleeper, she thought. She often wondered where his mind drifted off to when he closed his eyes. He seldom had a quiet night, and would often say that he could feel the wheels churning in his head as he tried to fall asleep but he would recall few details by morning time. The perils of the job, he would surmise.

Lately however, he was fastidiously asleep before his head could find a comfortable spot on the pillow. Was he truly at peace or simply medicated? The former, she had hoped.

"What is my problem?" she thought. "This should be the prime of our lives and our relationship, yet I feel so out of sorts; like this could unravel at any moment." Little did she know the true extent of her thoughts and her fears.

Her worst nightmares lurked in her very, very near future.

She hesitated but finally made her way to the car and rapped on the window until he woke up. A startled Bill gathered himself and reflexively, his collection of papers on the front seat and tried to exit the car. Kelly blocked his way as he tried to sidestep her.

"Not even a hello? Not even a kiss?" Sheepishly, Bill acquiesced and half-heartedly pecked her on the lips and inquired about her day as he made his way into the house.

The house smelled like it used to years ago—as if they were expecting company. It'd been a while since dinner was not out of a white take-out container. What gives?

She entered behind him and they exchanged pleasantries and they both retired to the kitchen. Bill fixed a Martini and Kelly spoke incessantly about her day at the country club, all of her various community projects, and her shopping excursions. Bill offered her a Martini, hoping to break her soliloquy. "No thanks," was the reply as she continued with her rants.

Bill raised an eyebrow. No Martini? What on earth does she need a sharp mind for? 'What do you have up your sleeve little girl?' was the look on his face.

Kelly smirked as she sensed that she had him off guard, one of a few times in like, forever!

"Careful," she thought, "too early to tip your hand."

Seemingly unfazed, Bill attempted to set her Martini glass on the counter. His gaze was diverted to the feast she had on the stove and he missed the countertop all together. The glass broke and cut a nice gash on his left hand.

She quickly grabbed a towel and attempted to wrap his hand.

Always the self-sufficient person, Bill took the towel from her hand wrapped the gash himself and disappeared towards the bathroom located around the corner to the left.

He washed his hand and took inventory of the cut. It was a nice gash, but it appeared to have missed anything important. He searched the medicine cabinet and located the appropriate sponges and cleaners and nursed his hand to the best of his abilities.

Kelly carried on with dinner and a perplexed Bill retired to the den with a bandage on his hand. He thumbed through the stack of bills on the table, eyed the shopping bags in the corner, and continued to the couch in his haphazardly constructed man cave, his favorite spot in the house.

All was seemingly well on his end and she didn't seem to be on the verge of rescinding her divorce truce.

Bill got comfortable and Kelly again went on about the rest of her day, even though he was well out of her eyesight. Her voice was reminiscent of the teacher in the Charlie Brown stories-purposeful but undecipherable. Bill flipped on the TV and went through most of the news and sports channels before giving up on seeing anything useful. He turned the TV off and switched on the CD player loaded with Phoebe Snow, his favorite. Kelly often asked why he liked her kind of blues so much. He would say that he needed to simply know that somebody had it worse than he did. She would laugh but never quite understood that he was referring to the two of them. He always wondered what would happen if she ever truly listened to the lyrics and heard her life play out in front of her.

Bill reached over and gathered the LA Times. He still kept up with the news from his former home 10 years removed; his training and best days were spent in Santa Monica, CA. He was never sure as to why he even bothered every night with this ritual since they always ended up the same way; fast asleep in no time, not recalling a single word he read. He was not wrong. Once again, his mind drifted as he made his way to sleepy land.

"SHIT," was his response to the faint tone of his pager he had conveniently left in the bathroom. Reluctantly, he got up, retrieved it, located the cordless phone, and returned the page.

# Chapter 3

Bill was once again submerged in his own little world as he pulled out of his driveway and into the side streets, heading back to the hospital. He often wondered what he would do if he didn't have himself as his best friend to talk to. "What is wrong with me? Why was I this way?"

He'd like to think that his profession made him into this cold, calculating son-of-a-bitch that he'd become but the reality is that he could trace this monumental shift in him to one event and one event alone.

"I used to be a social butterfly in college," he reflected. "I've grown to loathe small talk and fake friends. Can't trust anyone!"

He could count on one hand minus two fingers how many folks he could truly call a real friend these days. Kelly used to be on top of that short list until that faithful day three years ago when she accidently left her email account opened on the house computer. His better side told him to simply close it but his fragile and inquisitive ego told him to forge on. Much to his dismay, there was way more information than he cared to see.

That Fucking Whore!

Emails after emails corroborated her inexplicable absence from the house, day and night; Bill felt the gut-punch all the way through his psoas muscles as he read her prolonged and inappropriate exchanges with none other than Jim Branch, the CEO of the hospital, his now ex-best friend. "All that crap happened right under my nose." He started to relive that faithful day in his head again and shook it off but he couldn't help himself, so he continued.

"Now that makes two off my 'friends list,'" he thought. "That fucker recruited me to this shithole hospital. All the while, Ugh! I was an idiot. He begged me to stay after I received a lucrative offer from the East Coast. It's not me he really wanted here after all. He always had it bad for Kelly; I didn't know that he never stopped loving her. I sensed that, but I always assumed that his infatuation was more out of respect for me, us…

"We grew to be best of friends from the days I started dating her; the three amigos we were often called by those who liked us and the three amigas by the rest. Jim was the first person I told about that magical day when I met Kelly. I confided in him, in retrospect, more than I should have. He can recount the years and stories before we were married, better than I can, the different locations, positions that Kelly and I had sex at the hospital and about town. He would gleefully hang on to every word I spoke as I recounted her screams and distinctive moans. We fucked everywhere; in the library, the call rooms, the Operating Rooms, and best of all, my favorite golfing hole at the Sand River Country Club; nowhere was off limits to us. I remember that pervert watching us having sex while perched on the front of my golf cart; my pants were wrapped around my ankles, her skirt was hoisted up above her navel and her top was thrown over her head, exposing her voluptuous breasts. He was there; granted, it was I who told him about my plans. He watched the whole scene play out live in front of him. I saw him masturbating in the bushes. I'm pretty sure Kelly saw him too; being seen was part of the thrill for us. That bastard played me!!!

"Kelly and I were two insatiable fuck rabbits back then and Jim heard about it all.

"I still wonder how far back the two of them started this affair." He thought. He'd never pressed her for an answer.

"There wasn't a thing Kelly wasn't up to trying or to experiment with. I used to joke with her that the only thing left to do was to have group sex with her ICU sisters and maybe with small animals. To my chagrin, the emails confirmed that all that truly remained on that list were just the small animals; she enjoyed the company of the ICU staff, apparently both males and females," he thought. The only thing he couldn't corroborate was whether the ICU parties preceded the marriage or not; he simply didn't have the stomach to read all of the emails. No matter, he still could not shake off those images from his consciousness of her being such a kinky liar.

"In all fairness," he thought, "I probably screwed more than half those same girls myself over the years; even after I graduated and got married."

Funny how they both suspected as much but neither one had concrete proof until these one-sided damn emails.

Bill mentally recounted the many rounds of golf he played with Jim; the many dinners and barbeque parties at their respective houses. They've traveled the world, partaken in sexual tryst-sometimes with the same girl, at the same time and called each other brother and yet Jim would betray him at this level. Jim married in the interval; a beautiful blonde from the Ukraine. "Sweet revenge though, I fucked her right in his own bed that same night I read those damn emails," he reminisced.

As great a tussle as it was, sex with her did not make up for the betrayal he felt from Kelly, Jim. A bittersweet revenge, he thought as those thoughts still pierced right through him three years later. What good is it if he was the only holder of the whole truth? He could not bring himself to broach the subject with any of the parties involved.

Truth be known, he regretted that move even before he angrily ejaculated all over her, the pillows and the headboard. His facial expression betrayed him as he quickly dismounted her, dressed and left the house. They've never spoken of that day since.

The relationship between the wives was never the same after that. He often wondered if they had compared notes along the way. He and Jim's relationship frosted a bit but he wasn't sure if he was the architect of that discord. Bill can almost match all her interludes with times he simply didn't care where she was as long as she was out of his hair. He never even entertained the thought that sweet little innocent Ms. Kelly would step out on him like that. Still, he remained deeply conflicted about it all. They'd yet to have a conversation about it and he had pretended that he was not perturbed by it anymore. One late night after a few Martinis, he attempted this elusive conversation but she saw it coming from a mile away and countered him with a 'You really want to go there Mr. who fucked his way through every town and hospital we've ever been at?' look and he would cower away.

On most days, he vacillated from calling her escapades a well-deserved retribution to thinking that his marriage was a sham and he married a whore; he still couldn't resolve that conundrum.

They'd stumbled their way to the brink of a divorce—she having filed a month or two ago and just as suddenly, reversed course and called it off. She had been inexplicably friendly and amorous of late. He recalled the saying, "you can always change a woman's mind but you're just not sure for how long." He was still waiting for the other shoe to drop.

Bill's thoughts reverted back to earlier at the house. He actually enjoyed himself. This was not exactly what he had expected, he thought, as he sped away, again reminding himself of the earlier speed traps. Were they still there at this hour?

"We'll soon find out," he said out loud, as he recalled the many citations in his glove compartment.

"Memo to self," as he pantomimed talking to the hidden microphone in his collar, "call Commissioner Brookins' office to clear up these latest traffic digressions before I get pulled over again. There are but so many ways my good friend can protect me."

Back to real time, Bill replayed the events of the evening. There have not been many such quiet nights—or efforts at quiet—in the past two years or so. He actually did look forward to this one. "Yeah right!" He chuckled.

Kelly had yet to forgive him for all of his unexplained nights out, nights away from her, and presumably, the hospital also. Things would seemingly go well for a while until, rightfully so, he admitted; a sense of mistrust overcame her despite her best effort to thwart it.

Bill was never the type to ease her fears. "It was a small price to pay for not paying attention to the details early on in the marriage," he would say, "never mind the lies and her affair, at least the one I now know about, but have always suspected more. I'm not so sure whether I'm simply going through the motions to protect my assets, or do I actually have any feelings left for her. All that I know, as the song says, 'It's cheaper to keep her.' So, I'm keeping her for now."

He confronted Jim one day, though he has little recollection of that night as they were pretty wasted after an intense negotiating session with the hospital staff at a retreat in Reno.

The two of them were the last to leave the bar and Bill, who was still simmering from those damn emails brought up the subject. Two bottles of scotch later, a split lip on him, a shiner on Jim, umpteen overturned tables, strewn decorative vases and tableware, and the security and the restaurant staff eventually separating them were all they had to show for it.

With a promise to behave themselves and make the appropriate restitution of course, they resumed what turned out to be an enlightening conversation for the both of them.

Much to his surprise, Bill found out that Jim and Kelly were quite the item until he summarily stole her from Jim.

She was smitten with this young and brash Dr. Presser and Jim begrudgingly relegated himself to 'ex-boyfriend' status shortly thereafter. Much became clearer in that conversation. "Had Jim and Kelly hid it well, or did I simply and arrogantly never looked for it?"

In retrospect, he can't really say that they actually had an affair but they had remained best of friends even though Jim still pined for her. "Why didn't they or anyone tell me about the early connection?"

The answer was rather simple. Everyone assumed he knew and never brought it up. The reality was that Bill and Kelly were so quickly in love with each other and all seemed so natural at the time that a conversation about an old fling was never necessary or practical.

During the conversation however, Bill never fessed up to sleeping with Jim's wife. He suspected that Jim knew that something transpired; real or by reputation. Jim nonetheless managed to suppress his resentment and had remained professional through today. Their relationships cooled over the years and neither one could figure out how to move on from or own up to those events.

Admittedly, Bill was still angry, angry at the way the marriage turned from its inception. He had yet to explain or accept it.

Jim still harbored some resentment towards Bill for stealing his girl. Jim thought, "I should have stayed in Medical School and I'm convinced that she could have been my trophy wife if I had not bailed out after my internship year. She was so disappointed in me and the relationship fell apart not long after that. I've done well in the interim but I'm not quite the success that Bill is."

Bill's many sexual exploits, real or perceived, at the hospital are really the root cause of her cooling off from him. He tried to behave every now and then but admittedly, he has failed her miserably at being a faithful husband. If an affair truly existed, Bill had to admit that he was the one who drove her to Jim's arms, and Lord knows whom else's.

Bill continued with his trek through yesteryears. He and Kelly were quite the lovebirds when they first met that blissful day in the ICU. Bill was so smitten at first sight that he had to remind himself to breathe before he passed out from hypoxia. She noticed the effect she had on him and smiled and quietly looked away. He caught a slight glimpse of that look and felt his knees buckle as he sensed that the feeling could possibly be mutual. As confident of a vulture he could be when it comes to flexing his sexual prowess, Bill was the total opposite when he felt vulnerable. It was strange how different he could be. It was so inexplicable how it happened; one minute he was in total control and the next minute he was struggling to stand upright. That had happened to him one other time before. Amanda was the love of his life at seventeen until she caught him in bed with the next-door neighbor to the right of his house. In the words of Amanda, she was glistening as she clutched Bill, legs way up in the air, all the while screaming out his name and all kinds of vulgarity as she urged him to fuck her harder as she hung on for dear life. Bill's reassurance to Amanda that this tramp meant nothing to him fell on deaf ears as she continuously bawled at him.

"She was fucking screaming and glistening Bill! I never glistened with you dammit," was the last thing she said. She then shrieked something indecipherable. He tried to follow her but was soon met by her father on their front lawn of her house to the left of his. Her father's menacing demeanor was enough to force Bill to call it a day and retreat back to his own house.

He tried to reach her but gave up several months later as he watched her parents load their sedan and take her to an undisclosed University. Her absence left an indelible imprint on him that he had been trying to duplicate ever since; all to no avail until that faithful day when he ran into Kelly in the ICU.

"Aw Shit!" Bill exclaimed. "What an ass I've been," he muttered recalling Kelly's earlier gleeful mood as he dialed his home number.

Ring. Ring.

"Hi Babe," he said through a phony grin. "You forgot to tell me the surprise. Well? You can't keep me guessing. No! I probably will spend the rest of the night at the hospital," was his response as she promised to tell him upon his return.

"It's already late," he continued, hoping to con her into telling him over he phone—lessen the blow, he thought.

"No sense me driving all the way back home only to turn right back around in an hour or so in the morning. You know how grumpy I can get when I'm sleep deprived." He chuckled but he wasn't sure how well that was received.

Bill, ever the opportunist, had already made up his mind to return home tonight. However, he wanted all options left open and to keep her off guard as much as possible. If he didn't show up, it'll be business as usual but if he returned, she would be elated.

"No. I guess not," she replied as she sunk, deflated into the pillows on the oversize sofa in the den while gently nursing what was left of that bottle of dry sherry she had opened earlier. "No sense you coming back only for little ole me," she whimpered to herself as the phone went silent.

"I wonder if his reply would be different if he knew that I was carrying his child?"

"Doubtful," was the resounding thought. "Bill only does what's convenient for Bill. No more, no less. Someway, somehow, I'm going to have to make this decision on my own. We've (I've) prayed for this child for the longest time. Now I'm not so sure I want to carry his baby."

How funny these thoughts sounded to her. "Once upon a time, I worshiped the very ground that man walked on. Now I'm drinking myself into oblivion, running out of excuses not to abort his child."

Kelly clutched the pillows tightly as a tiny tear, the precious few that she had left, trickled down her face.

This seemed to be her favorite position of late, at home wondering with whom her man is being his loving and charming self to.

Of course, she never wanted to know the answer to that question. She wasn't sure whether to pity, envy, or just simply hate all of those women who have captivated her husband, just as she once did.

"Oh! So many times I wanted to confront him. I'm not so sure, which would hurt the most; knowing that someone else truly took my place or that my prime competitor was the person I wanted the most, Bill himself."

Sleep came a little easier tonight. A combination of sleep depravation over the past few nights, the relentless work she'd put into the dinner tonight, her shopping spree, the pregnancy, and of course, the alcohol she'd consumed. She managed to drag herself to bed and undressed in case he actually returned home and wanted to ravish her body again. Ironically, that was how she got pregnant. As she recalled the steps of that night, she gleefully relived the passion from Bill; a passion she had not felt in a long time. The bedroom was hotter than normal after a lengthy steamy shower that faithful night two months ago. Not anticipating his return, she bypassed the negligee drawer that he liked so much and went straight to bed, naked to all her glory. To her surprise, he showed up some hours later with just the right amount of drunkenness and kissed her softly at first and then proceeded to take her, take her in every which way possible; she offered very little resistance. So what if all that attention was meant for someone else; she nonetheless enjoyed every minute of it.

Tonight, like most nights, sleep came easy. She was soon lost in her comfortable world, a world where she seemingly controlled all the players, elements, and events.

Bill was surprised by how quickly he made it back to the hospital. The front entrance to the parking lot however, was cordoned off and he had to reroute himself all the way around the hospital complex to the rear entrance. Bill was not amused. He finally pulled into his familiar parking space; no small feat with all the new construction going on. The hospital was in the midst of a massive expansion project, which when completed, will triple its original footprint. Some, Bill included, albeit for different reasons, had even petitioned to rename the hospital as a way to distance themselves from its not so glorious past. Bill never confided in anyone that the name William Anthony Presser Medical Center would have a nice ring to it.

Fortunately, some things remained the same as he pulled into his available parking spot. He patted, in the usual and customary way, the sign at the head of the space that read, "Reserved, William A. Presser, M.D. Chairman Department of Anaesthesiology" as he passed it on his way to the main entrance of the hospital. This routine was simply a reminder that he was seemingly connected and belonged in this world.

Since he was closer to the OR than the dressing room, Bill decided to go see the patient before heading off to the Doctor's on-call rooms to change out of his rain-soaked clothes and into his OR scrubs.

Taking the stairs two at a time, Bill arrived in no time in the operating room suite. He scanned the bank of charts on the wall and grabbed that of Betty Robinson, a fifty-five year old lady with a perforated colon.

"It's probably cancer," he thought. Bill was incensed that the chart was incomplete. He therefore bypassed the routine pre-operative interview as planned and simply tossed the chart back towards the rack. Of course it missed and clanked off the metal bars and landed on the floor; the 'O' rings opened, strewing its contents all about. Hearing the commotion, the Circulating Nurse, Lisa, poked her head through the sliding glass doors separating the office from the hallway. She barely caught glimpse of someone disappearing through the exit doors. Judging by the antics and the size of the individual, she surmised that it was none other than the legendary Bill Presser. Than again, it could have been any of the other God-like assholes in the department.

"So much for efficiency," Bill thought as he headed for the call rooms.

This delay, however, would give him ample time for a detour, to the lounge, a much needed trip to the head, swallow a cup of coffee, and of course equally as important, just enough time to flirt with any available nurse in the lounge. I need a new conquest, he thought.

To his chagrin, the lounge was empty so he treated himself to a cup of Joe and made his way to the on-call room to finally change out of his wet clothes.

It is an unspoken rule and most doctors are superstitious and repetitive enough in their routines to expect to use the same call room every time. His first three choices were not available—that ticked him off. He blew into the fourth room, only to find it seemingly occupied.

"Come in," came the voice from the bathroom through the whirling sound of a hair dryer.

He recognized the voice and froze in place.

The magnitude of the set-up befell upon him as a backlit silhouetted figure emerged from the back and confidently strolled toward him.

Vicky, looking quite differently out of the oversize scrubs that she likes to wear to hide her figure, was a voluptuous, five foot two, one hundred and ten pounds, soaking wet, honey colored mulatto from Slidell, Louisiana. She was every bit the stuff that wet dreams are made of.

Her Florence Nightingale cap, worn slightly askew and her protruding nipples were the first things to come to light. Her piercing hazel eyes followed and it was obvious by their intense glare that they meant business.

Next in the light was a wry smile that revealed a set of slightly parted rows of perfect dentition being caressed by a tauntingly inviting tongue. Her lips quivered at the attention they garnished.

In no time, she was completely in the light. She cooed as she sensed that he was contemplating turning on his heels—he didn't.

"Close the door," she said. "There's a draft blowing."

He concurred by the sight of her erect nipples that were beckoning him. He wanted to comply. However, the scene paralyzed him. The scent of the candles and incense in the room betrayed the possibility of spontaneity. This reeked of a set up and he fell right into it.

Never to be outdone, Bill replied, "I just assumed that you were happy to see me!" As he stared at her nipples protruding through her loosely donned camisole.

She smiled, looked down and cupped her firm breasts that were barely contained by her top.

She uncovered her left nipple and gently stroked it, first slowly down and then firmly up. Her nipple resonated to her touch and grew more erect as she was visibly more aroused by her own touch and his undivided attention. He swore he not only saw her nipples oscillate up and down at least three times in each direction, but he actually heard them as well. She bent down and licked her nipple ever so softly as she maintained his unwavering gaze. She may not know how he truly felt about her but she was never unsure of the effect her eroticism had on him. Her eyes traced the contour of his heaving chest, down to his crotch. The rain soaked clothes accentuated his athletic physique. Again, she smiled.

"I can see that you are equally as happy to see me too," she said. "Come in baby." Then she whispered softly, "Close the door, love!"

He did as he was told this time; he had no choice. His body lacked much coordination and speed. He made it all the way in and leaned back against the closing door.

Her stroll resumed. She wore a matching garter and panties set that clung to her as if they took their job of caressing her body very, very seriously. Her naval ring flashed as a ray of light crossed her body. Her muscular legs glistened; wonderful set of pick-up-sticks, supported by a pair of three-inch Jimmy Choo black pumps.

The walk was unabashed and purposeful. She closed the gap, enough to smell the Grey Goose emanating from his flared nostrils. The kiss, barely felt, was sensed by every fiber in his body. He stood there, erect in every sense of the word.

"Check mate," she thought.

What was he supposed to do? Time—he translated everything into time.

"They're waiting for me upstairs in the OR," he thought. "This could get ugly," he admitted to himself.

She sensed the hesitation on his part. Unfazed, she forged ahead.

Being late for surgery was unacceptable. Yet, he allowed her to slowly undress him. He could not rush this seduction.

"I have to change out of these wet clothes and into my scrubs anyway," he rationalized to himself.

He meant to object, but remained rigid and paralyzed, enjoying the stimulations sensed by all his nerve endings. The cold air blowing on him from the overworked AC unit was a stark contrast to her warm breath on his chest.

Her eyes revealed a determined, beautiful, passionate side of this diminutive person. No one else knew this side of her; she was a woman who could suspend the passage of time. "Information overload, I'm about to blow," he thought so he closed his eyes, hoping to dampen his responses. Wrong again, as he felt this volcano that initially welled up from his toes but was now gathering steam in a rapid and upward motion, just past his ankles, heading towards his loins.

His proprioceptors were of no use to him as his knees buckled. He heard and felt her rhythmic breath trace a path of light, wet, and sensuous kisses in its wake, all the way down to his now throbbing penis. She had his arms lightly pinned to the door; he did not resist.

She let go.

He did not move.

She grabbed his penis with both free hands and stroked him closer to her face, inhaling every scent of him.

The image evoked in his mind, and the warmth of her tongue as she took all of him into her mouth without hesitation was more than he could stand. Never to be confused as an average-sized man, she'd been the only woman ever to accommodate his full girth and length down her throat without so much of a reflexive gag. His body jerked forward as he felt himself on the verge of coming in under a minute flat. He bent over, not exactly by choice and managed to corral her into his arm, spun her around, lifted and pressed her against the door with her legs draped over his shoulders. He held both of her wrists at arms length against the door.

She looked down at him again and smiled. She was more than willing to surrender to him.

He leaned into her, full of passion, snorting her aroma mixed with the fragrance she had bathed in. "Cabotine de Gres I believe, my favorite," he thought. He instinctively darted his tongue in and out of her, all the while appreciating the intensifying sweet aroma of her love canal. He wore her wetness like a mask on his face. She moaned and writhed against the door, quietly begging for more. She was unbelievably wet and ready for him. In one motion, he backed away and slid her body down the door as he stood up; licking his way past her clitoris, her naval and resting on her right erect nipple. He bit into it and stayed awhile, enjoying himself. He bit her harder and harder. It was a game they played. How much of this could she stand before she screamed out loud, begging him to stop or continue? She was a trouper this time. He sensed that he was hurting her. Yet, she pulled his head into her bosoms as her legs wrapped tighter around his waist.

He was the first to cry 'uncle' as he released her nipple from its dental captor. She cringed and dug her nails in his back as her raw nipple painfully glided past his razor sharp teeth. He smiled. She bent over and whispered, "Chicken," into his ears.

"What's the matter baby? You're afraid someone might hear me scream? Or is it you who can't handle the racket?"

She pulled away before he could construct a smart-ass response. He smirked and continued upward.

The taste of her right ear lobe was met by a convulsion that he recognized all too well.

Her downward migration down the door was enthusiastically countered by his penetration in a location she has previously referred to as his rightful place to be.

Her nails dug harder into his back as she held on for dear life. She let out what started out as a faint grunt that quickly escalated into a shriek that would have summoned all the gods from yesteryears if he had not covered her mouth with a free hand.

He heaved into her with all his might, wondering how this little girl can take all of him.

"You're hurting me," she meant to say. But, nothing came out. She gripped him harder, powerless to do anything else. His full weight had her pinned against the door.

She'd have to voice an objection at a later date as they released a powerful and rhythmical orgasm that had both of them collapsing down to the floor in unison.

As if on queue, both of their pagers went off simultaneously.

He let go of her and struggled to reach for his pants as she rolled her eyes, knowing exactly who it was that was paging them.

"Playing second fiddle to that damn pager again," she thought. "How many good orgasms has that pager cost me? A great form of birth control or what?" she quipped.

Having caught their respective breaths, Bill realized that he nearly trampled her as he made his way to the telephone on the desk. He shrugged a weak apology and continued to the desk and automatically dialed the main OR number.

"OR, this is Lisa," said the voice at the other end.

"Hey Lisa!"

"Dr. Presser? Are you joining us for surgery tonight? Well! Dr. Williams has been here for over an hour, pacing the floor wondering where you are!"

"Tell him to fuck himself or to start without me. No?—He can't do either one by himself? Well one of these days you'll have to show him how well you can do both."

He felt Vicky's penetrating glare on him as those words left his mouth. She knows all too well how much he loves to watch her play with herself. Now, she guesses that he likes to watch Lisa too. "Whom else does he watch?" she thought.

"Well then. I guess he'll have to wait won't he?"

"Yeah! Yeah! Tell him to dig his panties out of his ass. I'm changing and I'll be up shortly."

"How romantically ironic," Vicky thought, "this man has run out on me, more often than not. I have not been able to enjoy the perks of fucking his brains out then cuddling safely into his arms. I love the way he rolls over and quickly falls asleep and snores ever so gently after he comes. How much more vulnerable can a man be than immediately post coitus? He should be happy that he's still useful to me; otherwise he wouldn't stand a chance. They wouldn't even find the body," she added with a smile. She had uttered those words to herself on so many occasions that she's beginning to believe them. She shook her head and gathered her ensemble, strewn about the room.

"Live to fight another day," is my battle cry. Let him go; I'm sure I will still be on his mind, and all over him for that matter, well after his surgery." He quickly changed and made his ways to the OR, taking the stairs, this time barely one at a time.

# Chapter 4

The air seemed thick as Bill walked into the operating room. Dr. Williams glanced at the clock on the wall as Bill attempted a lighthearted chat with him. Bill came close enough to Angelica, the Scrub-Nurse, from behind that he almost contaminated her. He leaned in and pecked her on the nape of her neck. She would have objected, but, than again, it was Dr. Presser. Any one else would have been subjected to sexual harassment charges.

Dr. Williams grew more and more irritated by Bill's antics. Mrs. Robinson, the patient, was already on the table. Before Bill could go into his tirade, Maggie, another circulating nurse, much too old to be in the operating room, offered up a hush-hush explanation.

"Dr. Williams insisted that we bring her in."

"You know I don't give a flying rat's ass about that," was the almost simultaneous and loud reply.

"I know. I know," she continued in a soft and calming voice. "Rules are rules. But, you were not here and you know how difficult he can be."

Bill shot a look across the room that froze Dr. Williams; he made his point. Bill spun on his heels, grabbed the now completed chart and mumbled under his breath, "I'll be back," in his best 'Terminator' voice while raising his eyebrows a la Groucho Marx.

He headed back to the nurse's lounge where he found the same day-old pot of coffee and some fresh doughnuts on the back table; he helped himself to both.

As much as he liked to skirt the rules and regulations, Bill insisted that every one else follow his quirky ways. One would never guess that Bill was as old fashioned as it gets. He still insisted on greeting every patient, preferably in their room or the pre-op area, by their surnames or 'Sir or Madame" along with a firm handshake. He detested greeting patients for the first time on the OR table and especially from behind a mask to boot. "Not a nice way to endear yourself to the jury in case of an adverse outcome in the operating room," he always harped to the nurses.

He parked himself on the sofa, as he leafed through the now completed and voluminous chart of Mrs. Robinson. As he did, he caught a faint odor of Vicky under his fingernail. He thought about getting up and washing his hands but thought better of it and bit his nails instead.

He enjoyed them so much more than what turned out to be stale doughnuts and the day old coffee.

He smirked in amazement on how he could go from totally pissed off to completely amused in a split second. Vicky could do that to him too; Kelly on the other hand lately, not even close. When did that change? He didn't bother replying since the answer had been and will always remain the same. "Ever since she allegedly fucked my best friend!"

It was 'allegedly' because she never fessed up to it nor has he ever asked.

He glanced at the H&P, History and Physical exam report in the chart and got the gist of the case. Poor lady. A perforated viscous usually meant a colostomy bag for some time. If she were a mean-spirited person, it would probably be temporary. But, if she was a sweetheart of a person, it would probably be permanent—Cancer! Only nice people get cancer; jerks live on forever. I will go on indefinitely, he smirked.

Bill made his way back to the OR, and was instantly perturbed to find Vicky setting up his Anesthesia table.

"My case or yours?" was his greeting.

"Hello to you too Dr. Presser," was her response. "I was in the office finishing some paper work when this case came in. I thought I'd give you a hand. I can leave if you'd like," she said.

No response.

He grated his teeth as he glanced at all of the drawn and labeled syringes atop the anesthesia cart. More superstition, during an elective case, Bill does not trust any medication in any syringe drawn by anyone else but himself. He scooped them up and attempted to toss them in the sharp box marked 'used needles.'

"What's the matter honey? You don't trust me?"

He hates it when she calls him that, in public.

Fearing a prolonged argument, Bill acquiesced and replaced the syringes on top of the cart. Nonetheless, he still fumbled through the Anesthesia Cart drawers for more syringes and needles to replace hers in time. He attempted to draw up new medications all the while ignoring Vicky's banter. With reluctance, he abandoned his task and retrieved Vicky's syringes and turned his attention to Mrs. Robinson. With deft precision, he introduced himself and soothed her, after pulling down his mask and flashing her a million dollar smile. He induced her to sleep with Vicky's drugs and intubated her with a 7.0 ETT, Endotracheal Tube. He checked for bilateral breath sounds and flipped the pop-off valve on the Anesthesia machine that placed her on the mechanical ventilator. Her heart rate and blood pressure shot up immediately in response to the trauma of intubation. All of the alarms on the anesthesia machine followed suit and sprang to life. Perturbed, he didn't see that response coming and he instinctively treated both with Labetalol, a Beta-Blocker—a medication known for countering the effect of an accelerated heart beat and elevated blood pressure which is commonly referred to as the fight or flight response. In no time, all quieted down as Maggie began the abdominal prep with a Betadine solution used to kill all the bugs on the surgical field.

"So, you're going to ignore me for the rest of the night? You've already forgotten what happened thirty minutes earlier?" She said.

"I can still feel you inside of me love; your cum is still dripping down my legs baby," she whispered into his ears. "Can you get this kind of love at home sweetie, or is she strictly a missionary position, 'Wham-Bam thank you Mam' kinda girl?"

Bill nervously continued with his routine, all the while attempting to ignore her but to his dismay, he could feel his erection bulging against his loose-fitting scrub pants. He wanted her again!

He immediately sat down. No one can see my excitement!

He inserted an NG, nasal-gastric tube to suck out the stomach contents. He turned on the heating blanket that rested on the patient's upper torso and reassessed the scene. He then reached over and turned on the radio, trying to drown out her nonsense but she pressed on. He returned to the cart to begin his charting and bumped right into her. With the radio on, she felt comfortable raising her voice.

"I can and I have made you happy Bill," she continued closer to his ears this time. "We could be like this every night—as soon as you get rid of HER. You've promised me that we would be together soon Bill."

"Why'd you call off the divorce?" She said tersely. "Let me guess. Prissy lil' ole Kelly promised to do better? Is that it? Don't you think that in no time it will be like days of old? She will frustrate you right back to my bed. Who are you kidding Bill?"

"Oh I get it!" She said playfully, "Do you have a better plan Boo? A permanent plan Bill? Can I help? Are you man enough to take care of this or do I have to take matters into my own hands?" She pressed on, her mood more cynical as she tried to divert his attention back to her.

Sensing that she wouldn't quit, Bill turned and said through gritted teeth, "I will take care of it OK! I told you that. I do have a plan. Now go," he said louder than intended. All in attendance stopped and looked their way.

Flushed with remorse, Vicky excused herself and the surgery resumed uneventfully. It was cancerous of course; he sensed that Mrs. Robinson must indeed be a nice person. The procedure was more arduous than expected. The cancer had consumed every possible tissue that it could find in the abdomen. There was no point in even attempting to resect any part of it so Dr. Williams announced to the room that this would be a lesser than expected procedure given the unexpected findings of widely disseminated cancer—a 'peek and shriek' as we call it in the business. Having said that, everyone in the room knew that Dr. Williams would heroically forge on, as he'd been known to do on too many occasions. He began the process of attempting to de-bulk the tumor. He knew it would not be curative but reducing its sheer size would give the patient a better quality of life, whatever she had left. The reality of it was that most tumors cause the most damage by their sheer size and bulk, interrupting normal function or simply syphoning enough vital nutrients from adjacent normal organs. Simply reducing their size would buy the patient some more quality time. He nipped here and there and of course as customary, caused more problems than he fixed. She began to ooze from every surface as he frantically tried to stem the tide of her bleeding out before his eyes. He managed to cauterize most of the opened vessels but had to admit that he had lost about three units of blood in the process; most surgeons usually underestimated the amount of blood they'd lost while in the throws of trying to save a life. So, Bill automatically added another half to a full unit to the total blood loss. In a healthy patient with a total of 5-7 liters, around 10-12 units of blood, that would have been manageable but Mrs. Robinson started out with only 3-4 liters at best in her system, this amount of blood loss would put her very close to death, closer than either doctor was comfortable with. All of her vital signs confirmed the danger she was in. Blood soaked sponges were collected on the back table and even the blood drawn for analysis began to look more like diluted Cherry Kool-Aid as opposed to its customary tomato juice color and consistency. Bill cursed Dr. Williams the whole while as he barked out orders, over the phone to the blood bank staff to type and cross her for 4 units of packed red blood cells and to stay four units ahead at all times he added; in addition, he also requested that they immediately send him 4 units of O-blood, the universal donor. She would not live long enough to receive her own crossed-matched blood; it was a task that normally would take another 20 minutes to complete but it was 20 minutes that she didn't have. He also requested a ten pack of platelets and another 2 units of FFP, Fresh Frozen Plasma for good measures. Deep in his heart, he knew this was an exercise in futility but he forged on, recalling the many times he was wrong. Besides, he was not ready to ruin his record of never loosing a patient on the OR table. He was always amazed at the resiliency of the human body to adapt. She didn't make it this far in life by being a pussy; was his saying whenever the crew had that look of despair, wanting to prematurely pull the plug. It was always a dichotomy between being a hero versus conserving scarce resuscitative resources for another salvageable patient.

Dr. Williams, satisfied that he'd done as much as he could, replaced the bowels in their respective places and promptly closed the abdominal cavity. As was sometimes the case, the peritoneal contents had expanded and didn't quite fit as they did prior to surgery. Once closed, the pressure in the abdomen was now transmitted directly to the chest cavity making ventilation, even mechanically, extremely difficult. By experience, Bill knew that even in a healthy strapping young man, it would be difficult for the patient to breathe on their own, let alone this frail, elderly woman. Besides, Bill's rule of thumb was to never extubate anyone after extensive abdominal surgery, especially in the middle of the night. That was a recipe for respiratory failure and a dead patient by morning. Plenty of lawsuits have been paid out because of that cowboy mentality that all will be ok if I pull the ET tube but no one has ever been sued for being conservative and leaving the patient on mechanical ventilation, at least overnight. The crew knew that ahead of time and ordered an ICU bed equipped with a ventilator for Mrs. Robinson.

For once, Bill was pleased. 'Membership has its privilege,' he was fond of saying. "I'm so fucking tired of explaining medicine 101 to amateurs," he thought.

Bill took Mrs. Robinson directly to the ICU; she had all the prerequisite tubes hanging from every possible orifice and then some. Before leaving the OR, Bill's conscience had the best of him. He inserted a CVP line in her Right Internal Jugular Vein in her neck. A CVP line is a glorified IV line, albeit much larger than the standard IV placed in the arm. Additionally, it can be more comfortable and longer lasting. Furthermore, many more hemodynamic parameters can be obtained from a CVP line, which in turn can better streamline the latest greatest state of the art therapy available. The nurses always praised him for such heroics, absolving them of the task of finding the next best vein to replace the last peripheral IV that barely functioned. He also placed an Arterial Line in the right wrist, in the Radial Artery to be exact. This would allow for continuous, beat-by-beat blood pressure measurements rather than the old fashioned and unreliable arm cuff readings garnered at best every two minutes; most patients hated the latter. One or the other task should get him a hug. He thought, "But both?"

Whoop Whoop!

"I may get laid," he smiled.

He settled her in her ICU cubicle, still intubated and sedated enough for the next 12 hours, he thought. He gave report to the crew and left ample instructions for more medications for pain, cardiovascular support, sedation if necessary, and most of all, gave explicit directions not to call him under any circumstances. "I'm going home. Kindly refer all queries to the good Dr. Williams," was his parting quote as he attempted to slip out the door but not before he made his obligatory round and flirted with all the nurses in the ICU. He glanced at the clock, 12:39 that translated into a 3 hour doze at home, factoring the drive to and fro his domicile, the requisite chat with Kelly, and maybe a tussle before passing out on her.

He had a full schedule in the morning, which meant for another long and grumpy day. "Swell!" He thought as he emerged from the ICU with no particular destination in mind.

# Chapter 5

Kelly, fast asleep in her bed for what seemed like the past few hours was still clutching the bottle of dry sherry from dinner; she was startled by a noise that she did not recognize. Always the paranoid type. Kelly froze in place, waiting for something God-awful to occur—she always waited. Yet by morning, she never quite recalled when sleep overtook her obsession.

She placed the bottle on the nightstand and eased herself back under the comforter; slowly feeling her body, merge as one with the bed.

Again! The same noise, someone was in the room. That same sense of dread returned in full force. She knew for sure this time that it was not her imagination. She could feel it!

Someone had to be in the room. The half dubious look on her face foretold the countless other times she had been wrong. She tried to will herself back to sleep but that dire feeling remained. She scanned the room for any reassuring signs that her usual paranoia was again having the best of her. After all, she knew that she did have an overly active imagination. Bill said so himself. "I've been wrong on so many occasions," she thought.

This time however; she was right.

Before she could come to grip with her predicament, she felt two hands clamp down on her ankles, yanking her straight over the end of bed. Instinctively, she retracted at the hip and repetitively shot both legs in the direction of the hands. She continuously kicked violently until she felt solid contact on her assailant as the grips were simultaneously released.

Kelly frantically screamed and continued to kick with both feet while flailing with both arms as she tried to gain the upper hand, but no contact this time.

She sat up at the edge of the bed, her chest violently heaving for air. The room grew eerily silent except for the wheezing sounds emanating from her lungs.

She wasn't quite sure what to do next. "Scream? No one would hear me. Run! Which direction?" she thought.

She felt immobilized by her fear.

She waited. Her eyes darted back and forth over the entire room, which was softly lit by the nightlight from the bathroom, but she saw nothing!

The armoire looked menacing. Her collection of teddy bears on the rocking chair seemed like a thousand ghoulish monsters waiting to pounce on her. The leaky faucet resonated like echoing footsteps closing in on her.

The harsh taste of Adrenalin in the back of her throat and the pounding sensation in her chest, reminded her that this could not possibly be a dream but the stark reality that someone was in the room and they meant to do her harm.

"What is happening? Why me?" Admittedly, Bill crossed her mind—but why?

She never had a chance to ponder the question much longer as she suddenly sensed a much heavier weight than the actual beddings that encircled her. She felt trapped by the comforter as she tried to bunch it toward her for protection. She jumped up, trying to get out of bed and tripped over a bulky mass as she tried to make her way to the bathroom. She thought she heard a soft moan as she made contact with the same mass and ended up flat on her face. The comforter and the many pillows that are usually in her bed however, cushioned her fall.

"That's the fuck why I sleep with all of this shit on the bed!" she felt like yelling at Bill who had questioned her choice of beddings on so many occasions.

She realized that she must have injured her assailant as she tripped over him because no sound or movement came from beneath the comforter.

The room grew eerily quiet again—save of course, for her heavy breathing.

Lying on the floor, in between the bed and the dresser, Kelly once again slowly gathered the comforter and crawled towards the bathroom on her elbows and knees. She was panting so loudly that she failed to hear the storm gathering behind her.

Suddenly, without warning, Kelly felt a tug on the comforter. "Dear God," she thought, "let it be caught on the edge of the bed."

Wrong again.

She turned just in time to see the assailant's small yet recognizable surgical blade from her days as a scrub nurse in the OR, moving toward her at a speed she could not escape.

She momentarily lost sight of it in the dark but soon realized where it went as she felt the cool fluid run down the back of her legs. It was like nothing she would have imagined.

She felt the splitting of both heads of her gastrocnemius muscle on the back of her leg, but it was not painful; at least not until she instinctively retracted her leg.

That motion sent an excruciating electrical impulse to her brain that she wished she could ignore but couldn't.

It was followed by another slash and yet another impulse just as intense as the first. The books really lied! That shit really hurt. There may not be any pain fibers imbedded deep within the muscles, however, the many spindles on the skin more than made up for it. The excruciating signals from the C-fibers, the large nerve fibers that are responsible for transmitting pain sensation to the brain, screamed loudly and seared in her head.

Miraculously, she regained enough movement with her other leg to continue her escape towards the bathroom door. "Maybe just maybe I can reach the light switch," she thought, "I will not die in the dark. I will know the identity of my killer. I will confront him on the other side," she willed.

As her right hand made its way up the wall, she sensed the full weight of the assailant countering her every movements against the comforter that gave her a veiled shelter.

"My God, how much worse can this get?" she thought.

Fortunately, she never knew. Her last recollection would have been the burning sensation up her arm as her hand was impaled on the light switch with a number fifteen surgical grade steel blade that penetrated her hand all the way down to the knife handle.

She managed to turn the lights on but her eyes never registered another image. The lights turned off again as the weight of her body slumped down to the ground, leaving a trail of fresh blood on the wall.

Her body was still reacting, but her brain was already offline. Her assailant knew this.

She fought valiantly but her movements were more reflexive than purposeful. She was dragged back to the bed. She was laid in a supine position and her protective cover was removed, exposing her naked body. A mask was strapped over her face. The other end was attached via a tube to a Penthrane canister. This was followed by a forward jaw thrust to ensure a clear and unobstructed airway, thus allowing her to fully inhale the Anesthetic gas.

"She needs to breathe this in quickly before she awakens," thought her assailant. He definitely wanted her breathing and alive for what was to come next. Warm and salty bright red blood spurting from an open vessel was far more rewarding than cold dark and deoxygenated blood oozing from an open wound. With precision, the assailant proceeded to tie her to the four bedposts. Once secured, he took his time to admire her from her lovely golden locks down through her voluptuous figure. He enjoyed every inch of her from his vantage point above her as he appreciated her deep yet serene breathing pattern. Excellent!

He could feel his erection springing to life, restrained only by his taut pants.

"Can't be distracted," he thought.

He looked around and gathered the rest of his tools strewed about the head of the bed during his earlier tussle with Kelly. Ever the deliberate and skilled technician, he gathered and arranged his instruments on the nightstand in the sequence he would need to complete this task.

What followed was unimaginable.

He once again selected his favorite scalpel, admired it, appreciating it in his hand for the delicate yet lethal combination that they have become. He reminisced about the clumsy early days of his first few victims and patients and just as quickly returned to the present.

In one precise, deliberate and deep stroke made from her Xyphoid process down to her pubic bone, the contents of her abdomen were exposed and spilled out unto the bed. No need to be delicate, he thought.

She squirmed and moaned ever so softly as if he'd just mind-fucked her in his serene yet grotesque kind of way. He took notice that she was not totally asleep and smiled. The assailant inhaled deeply, soaking in every essence of her inners as he slowly reached into her abdominal cavity. He took his time to remove his top before proceeding. He manually palpated all of her internal organs and took delight in their contour, their softness and especially, the peristaltic movement of her bowels as he gently rubbed them against his torso. He noted the pulsation of her vessels in her mesentery as he reached deeper inside her to fondle her spleen to his right, her liver to his left and her pulsating Aorta deep within the abdominal cavity. He always thought she drank too much however, her liver felt very smooth and normal rather than the hard and knotty consistency of a cirrhotic alcoholic liver. Her bloated gallbladder, which rested below the liver bed would need to be removed now or maybe at a later point if she survives this, he thought as he palpated it between his forefingers. He paused momentarily, reached for the scalpel and thought better of it. No need to spill her gallbladder's contents but he contemplated doing exactly that; Greenish toxic bile would ruin this amazing view. He finally accepted that and opted to replace the instruments in the order he had set them earlier. He continued to examine inside her abdomen, all the way down into her pelvic cavity. The pleasurable warmth of her womb almost overtook him but he deferred and kept to the plan. On the way, he again felt the pulsation of her descending aorta as it bifurcates into the left and right common femoral artery. One nick, he thought, and her nectar of life would gush out in less than two minutes. Again, too messy, he thought, and continued. The urge to extinguish her life was raging within him but that was not today's mission; she had to live!

He paused at the uterus, caressed it in a seductive and sexual way and placed it on top of her intestines so he could take full visual pleasure in her center of fertility. He stepped back and admired it. He then reached down and freed her ovaries from deep within her pelvis, stroking them as the most precious thing he'd ever touched. He immediately sensed his everincreasing erection straining harder and harder against his pants. He continued to caress her uterus, pulled on the drawstrings and released his bottoms and allowed his cock to escape from its restraints. He felt the urge to release right then and there but paused long enough to slip on a condom and position her so he could look into her eyes, glazed and all, the moment he shot his load deep inside her. Instinctively, he suddenly gathered himself, sensing that something was horribly wrong. His brain, understandably preoccupied with the task at hand, managed to finally register that something was afoul and he froze in place.

Something was off, he thought again. He returned to the uterus. It was much larger than expected; its contour felt odd—That's not possible! How could I miss that? Her womb had the unmistakably feel of a gravid uterus and ovaries. He has touched other victims like this but they were deliberate selections.

"Yes!" he exclaimed to no one. "I know this feeling. She's definitely pregnant," his brain alarmed!

"Fuck me to no end!" He screamed out loud.

Surprisingly, he immediately felt remorseful and ill. A wave of nausea overcame him. Before he could compose himself, his abdomen heaved and spilled all of its contents all into her abdominal cavity.

"This has gone terribly wrong. It was not suppose to be like this," he thought. He was not aware that she was pregnant and now, he was on the verge of taking an innocent life, the fetus; he didn't give a fuck about her wretched existence. The ramifications were more than he could comprehend at this time. "Think!" he screamed at himself.

He inhaled deeply and composed himself as he gathered all of his tools. Concentrate! He cursed deeply under his breath and tried to focus on the task at hand. He was upset at his miscalculation but more so at his amateurish reaction to the events as they unfolded. This was not part of the plan. Can he improvise while completing his objective? "Options were what again?" he thought.

He managed to control himself all the while reworking the plan in his head and, as he progressed, he felt his receding hard-on once again spring back to life. He smiled and calmly spread her legs and in a deliberate and continuous motion, he thrusted himself deep into her. Sadly, she did not react. He realized in all this commotion that he forgot to adjust the Penthrane and the gas mixture she inhaled was higher that he would have liked. She was in effect under a deep level of anesthesia.

Fuck! Nothing was going according to plan but despite his many failures tonight, his body was enjoying the moment. He jerked violently as he ejaculated his entire load into her. He paused long enough to admire his accomplishment. He then slowly withdrew; carefully removing the condom he had managed to slip on, without spilling any of its contents and tossed it in his bag. He then meticulously gathered his tools as she lay there motionlessly but more importantly, still breathing. He continued to the bathroom, laid out the tools on the counter. He washed the knife then replaced the blade, the tonsil clamps, the peons, the Cokers; the rest of his instruments. He counted them one by one; a complete surgical tray, all accounted for. He smiled.

He returned to the room and surveyed his work. "Well done!" He smirked. He was back in charge.

He checked his watch, twenty minutes off course. He cleaned up the scene, including the mess he made in her peritoneal cavity, as best as he could. He checked her pulse, thready but present. She was not long for this world, he thought. He reached over and exchanged the anesthetic gas she was inhaling with a pure oxygen mask. It was imperative that she survived this, at least for a few more hours. Ideally, she should wake up just in time to fully comprehend the situation she was in before slipping off into the afterlife.

He again surveyed and carefully staged the scene until he was satisfied that all the important elements were in place and he gathered all unnecessary pieces and placed them in his duffle bag. At the last minute, he spotted his top peering out from under her and yanked it with such force that she would have fallen off the bed if her arms weren't still tied to the bedpost. He reset the scene. He wanted the whole world to know that he had defiled the whore, the bane of his existence.

"Calm down!" he exclaimed through gritted teeth and finished the clean up. Satisfied, the last thing he did was to remove the Oxygen mask and restraints from her face and arms, respectively. "I must not let them in on all of my secrets. This must appear as if she was fully awake when I did all of this to her." He then proceeded to the front door unlocked it and once again surveyed his surroundings, retraced his steps, and exited as quickly as he'd appeared through the basement door. He again checked his watch, now 40 minutes longer than he had allocated.

"I must get back. I can't let my absence be noticed."

He took a circuitous route through the yard to avoid detection and made his way back to his truck parked down the street. Once inside, he closed his eyes and replayed the evening in his head. Everything checked out. He felt his hard on stir once again in his pants and almost returned to the house for a reprise but his better sense vetoed that thought. He reached in his glove box and picked out his burner cell phone and made an anonymous phone call. It would be fifteen, maybe twenty minutes at best before she would be discovered. He slowly pulled out into the street and to his surprise, he almost ran into a patrol car coming from the opposite direction. "Fuck! That Fast?" He screamed out and banged his hands against the steering wheel, activating the horn. Somehow he managed to regain his composure and slowly passed them as they exchanged a sideway glance. He continued and made the right turn and disappeared into the night.

Unbeknownst to him, Mrs. Henry, the nosy next-door neighbor had spotted his coming and going and called the authorities. She has always been intrigued with the peculiar behaviors of the Pressers, from Kelly's late night visitors to Bill leaving and returning at all kind of hours. In his favor, Mrs. Henry's eyesight is not what it used to be. She was not able to provide an accurate description of this strange truck but she thought that she had seen it before but was not quite sure of it, let alone the color or make and model.

Both officers immediately harkened back to the truck they just passed in the street and made note of it. They had a better sense of the descriptive nature of the truck but unfortunately, they could not correlate it to anything Mrs. Henry described. They wrapped up their interview with her and made their way to their next destination, the Presser's house where everything would come to light.

By morning, everything would indeed be in place.

# Chapter 6

Dr. Presser was awakened by a succession of loud raps on the door. As usual, it took several minutes for him to re-equilibrate to his surroundings. He gazed at the alarm clock on the desk, 05:12 A.M. The room seemed foreign to him. The background lights were in unfamiliar positions than he was accustomed to at home. He looked to his right for the bathroom nightlight and he saw nothing but darkness. He scanned straight ahead for what should be his bedroom door and again, pitch black. "What the fuck? Where am I?" he thought. Having had this sense of confusion on too many occasions, Bill paused and allowed his head to clear as he began to retrace his steps from the previous night. He quickly realized that he was at the hospital; the call room to be exact.

Still fuzzy, he had enough faculties about him to know that the person on the other side of the door was about to get the facial of their life. He looked around and located his scrub pants and laboriously donned them on. He stumbled towards the door, straightened up and regally yanked it open.

He expected a nurse, a housekeeper or at best, an intern who was up all night seeking a quiet space to regenerate before yet another grueling day. Instead, Dr. Gill Stewart, Chief of Staff, two suited detectives, and a spat of uniformed individuals greeted him; the former was with that 'say it isn't so' look about him.

Although confused on the inside, Bill's outward demeanor, by training, did not betray the bewilderment in his belly. His thoughts quickly turned to Vicky, "Were we that loud last night?" he thought. Surely, whatever the noise level was last night; it did not merit this level of scrutiny. "What can they possibly charge me with," he thought, "disorderly conduct? Having way too much fun?" He smirked. This last act did not sit well with the detectives and they both simultaneously stiffened.

"What in the hell is this?" His angry tone trailed off as he surmised that this might be more than he could have imagined. His posture hardened as he tried to appear more awake than he really was. Bill reached down and retied the drawstring on his scrub pants, a nervous move. He reached back and fumbled for his top that was on the chair nearby, donned it and ran his fingers thorough his bald scalp; still a habitual move from his hairy days. Satisfied that his outward demeanor was in order, he again inquired about the nature of this early morning visit.

"Dr. Presser?" said Detective Afoot, the lead detective to his left.

"Can you account for your whereabouts since you left recovery room at uh, 00:08?"

"I was in ICU then here," he responded in bewilderment.

"Yes!" said Detective White, the secondary detective to his right, as she flipped her notepad, searching for details or simply playing the stall game.

"You left around 00:30 and said you were heading home. When did you return here?"

"Uhm!" He thought for a while. "No! I changed my mind and came straight here. I've been here all night," was the terse retort through his confused demeanor. "Why all these fucking questions at this God-forsaken hour," he wondered.

Before he could fully comprehend the question, Detective White added, "Are you aware that your wife is currently in the ICU upstairs, barely alive?"

Dr. Stewart spoke next. "We've been calling you all night. Didn't you get all of our pages? Why didn't you answer?"

"My wife? ICU? What on hell are you talking about? Will someone make some God damn sense?" he yelled.

Bill's mind raced in a multitude of directions. He had no answers. Yet, he saw the gaze from beyond the door. Detectives White and Afoot waited impatiently for an answer while they assessed his demeanor. No words came through even though he tried.

"Woah, Woah. Back the hell up! Why is she in the Intensive Care Unit? What happened?" The weight of his question befell upon him, as he slumped back towards the bed. "Kelly is hurt," he thought, "and I was here with..." he silently thought.

He sobbed openly, searching for words, questions.

"What happened? Is she all right?" The detectives were not impressed and they again waited.

"I last saw her when I left for the hospital around 7:30 last night," said Bill. "She had something to tell me. She never got around to it."

"Why not," interrupted Detective White.

"We, uh, uh, we got side tracked—I got paged and returned to the hospital." Bill recounted the events as best as he could concentrate. "She was fixing dinner, I opened the mail, watched TV and my pager went off. See for yourself," he directed at the group, as he reached for his pager on his scrub pants, nothing.

He suddenly remembered that he has not seen his pager since… Vicky against the door, the returned call to the OR; it all came flooding back.

He receded to the back of the room and fumbled for his pager on his trousers; it was not there either. He hesitated and turned towards the door, scanning the room for his pager. Nothing! He reentered the room and searched his bed, tossed it about, no luck. He scanned the rest of the room. Still dazed, perplexed as his pager was nowhere to be found. He went through the drawers in the desk, nothing. He started for the bathroom when he suddenly heard the distinct buzz of an unanswered page emitting from the bed. He returned to the bed, quieted, and listened again. After a short interval, he heard the noise again.

He dropped to his knees and silently waited for the next buzz. There, towards the back of the bed, he traced the sound to his pager, just under the covers on the floor. He quickly retrieved it and scrolled through the many numbers on the small, elongated LCD screen. There were several entries with a 911 extension, and others that he did not immediately recognize.

"Here, see for yourself," as he shoved the pager towards the detectives. "The hospital first paged me at 19:22. I was home. I arrived in the OR at approximately 21:00." He lied, trying to fudge the time line.

He regretted that, knowing that some surveillance cameras were still operational even in the face of the ongoing constructions.

"Why so long," was the quick retort from Detective White, "for what I surmise, should have been a twenty-five minute ride with no traffic at that time of night?"

"Yes! He protested, there was traffic, there was a construction zone on Herndon and the garage was locked down and I had to go around through the back. And, uh, uh," he again thought about Vicky. Thought better of it and said no more.

"Correct me if I'm wrong Doctor" said Detective Afoot, "you reported to the OR at," he flipped though his notepad, "21:04. Can any one else account for your whereabouts from the time you answered the page to the next time you were seen in the OR? And for that matter, between the time you left the OR at uh 00:30 and now?"

Why all the questions? It suddenly dawned on Bill that his timeline was inconsistent. Someone must have seen him or heard him and Vicky's little tussle earlier. That both unnerved and irritated him to think that he was answering questions rather than attending to Kelly.

"Can we do this another time?" was his dejected response to the detective as the big uniformed personnel slowed his forward progress towards the posse.

"Cuff me, take me downtown or meet me at bedside" Bill snorted. "Why on God's earth are you asking me all of these fucking stupid questions?" A pregnant pause from the crowd was long enough for Bill to make up his mind.

"I'm going to see my wife." With that, he gathered himself and stormed out of the door with both detectives and uniformed personnel in tow.

He took the stairs, two at a time, all the way to the seventh floor. He tried to enter the ICU, but two cops whose massive physiques left very little room for him to squeeze through impeded his forward progress. Detectives Afoot and White arrived, out of breath, but just in time to keep him out of a body cast. With a nod from Detective Afoot, he was allowed to enter. The tension in the ICU was quite evident. They all were aware of the state of the Presser household, the affairs, the on and off again divorce and most damning of all, his late arrival here. Where the hell was he?

To all, on a good day, the next of kin is always suspect number one. Today, he was suspect one through twenty.

He had made this entrance on so many occasions, but under much different circumstances. As a resident, Bill always insisted on transporting all post operative patients destined for the ICU directly upstairs, bypassing recovery room, just so he can see Kelly, at first in her candy-striper outfit, and later in her nursing get-up that accentuated her every curve. "A woman in uniform," was the first thing he ever said to her with wobbly legs when he first saw her in the ICU so many years ago. Seemingly offended, she quietly chastised him without even batting an eye. Later on, as they lay in bed, she would confess how grotesquely charming she found him that day. She felt special even though every other woman in the ICU was in uniform. Thereafter, her heart would skip a beat every time the double doors flung open, hoping that it was he.

A jovial greeting for all present; nurses, critically ill patients and family members alike usually accompanied his usual entrance to the ICU. Not today. They all despised him—it was more like a deep-seated hatred they harbored towards him. Kelly was one of their own. That is, before she gave up on all of the hard work she did to achieve her degree to marry this ogre of a man. They all wished he could trade places with her—all except for Brenda.

Brenda was the overnight ward clerk, a fixture in the ICU for several decades. For some odd reason, she took a shine to him ever since he was a young intern, rotating at the hospital. Fresh out of Medical School, he was a brash, lanky yet cocky intern; unlike any other she has seen in her combined 20+ years experience. She knew of the love and admiration he and Kelly once shared. She always defended Bill during the many 'girls-only' chat sessions in the nursing lounge. It was always she and Kelly versus the rest of the crew. They both saw something in him that no one else could ever fathom. As the years passed, Kelly regretfully learned that many others in the hospital, including some of her colleagues in the ICU, also found the good Dr. Presser's charm equally irresistible. What he lacked in beside manner, he more than made up in clinical skills and his in-bed comportments. They hated him indeed, however, there was always a sense of comfort whenever he was at bedside. Dr. Presser can and will always save the day. That more than made up for his other worldly failings.

Bill hesitantly made his way to cubicle 4 where Kelly was being attended to by a team of 3 nurses, an attendant and the Critical Care Doctor on call, Dr. Stedman. Brenda reached out and squeezed his hands as he passed the nursing station. He smiled back, half-heartedly at her. He inhaled deeply and attempted to enter her room. The entire law enforcement team present and Dr. Stewart impeded his forward progress.

"What the fuck?"

"Sorry Bill. We can't let you in right now. You know from the past how sensitive an investigation like this can be," said the COS, Chief of Staff. "We can't allow you in for now Bill. You know it will be temporary."

Steaming, Bill closed his eyes and attempted to calm down; this can't be happening!

When he opened them again, Dr. Stedman, steps away from him; waited for signs that he was approachable when his eyes finally focused on them. Dr. Stedman quickly updated him in medical lingo. That shortened the extensive report on all that ails Kelly. He'd seen and heard worse before but he never quite made this kind of connection between a living human being and the blob lying in the bed in front of him, until now. He suddenly felt the weight of every patient's family member that he had dismissed in the past as cry fucking babies. Was it worse to be in the profession and know exactly how bad it truly was or to simply remain in the dark as a consumer? Either way, he surmised, it was much different when the shape in the bed is one of your own.

Brenda watched from the door. The shear pain he felt, she surmised, must be indescribable.

In a trembling voice, Bill asked Dr. Stedman "How is she really doing?"

"She's been through a lot," was the oversimplified response. "Considering that she was pulseless when we found her. It's a small miracle that she's still with us. However, we were unable to salvage the pregnancy; I'm sorry," said Dr. Stedman as he placed a sympathetic hand on Bill's shoulder on the way out of the door.

"Pregnancy? Baby?" He murmured.

For the first time, his look betrayed him. The nurses in the room realized that what Kelly had gleefully shared with them earlier in the day was all news to Dr. Presser. The pain in his eyes overcame most of the animosity they had harbored towards him. No one deserved this, they seemingly thought in unison. By shear sympathy, all present parted and allowed him in the room. He slowly approached the bed, reached for her hands and stroked it gently. She didn't respond.

He vacillated from the clinician, assimilating all of the numbers on the bank of monitors above, to the grieving husband, barely recognizing his wife. She was badly bruised and swollen; she was not recognizable as the beauty queen she once was. "How did my baby end up like this? Who, what monster exists who could inflict so much pain?" It was an all-new and incomprehensible sensation to Bill. He just stood there, stared, waiting for any movement, any signs of life from Kelly, but there was nothing. The tears flowed freely at first from Bill, then from all of the nurses and attendants.

Meanwhile, Detectives Afoot and White were continuously on the phone with the crime lab, the D.A.'s office and others, piecing together what seemed like a no-brainer of a case. The preliminary report on the blood samples from Bill's house came back with a definitive match for Kelly and an unknown, presumably the assailant.

"One guess as to whose do I think it is?" Said Detective White to Afoot. The bandage on Bill's hand was not lost on either of them.

Open and shut case, was the look on her face.

"Do you have a sample from the good doctor for a cross match?" She asked the technician on the other line. "As a matter of fact, we do have a sample but the chain of command is not well established," she was told. "However, we have enough to run a preliminary cross test. To be safe," the tech continued, "we will need to draw a fresh sample from the doctor, ASAP."

With several high profile cases that went sour over crime lab incompetence, it is understandable why Detective White hesitated. She was not ready to hinge her whole case with a rush to judgment on preliminary results. Still with that, Detective White decided to hedge her bet and sprung to her feet toward Dr. Presser. In a cold and seemingly sadistic maneuver, Detective White leaned over and whispered in Bill's ear, "You better have a good alibi or I'm gonna nail you for this, you son of a bitch! You better hope she lives buddy or this will go beyond attempted murder, the chair maybe."

Bill remained frozen in time as the words resonated in his ears. "Attempted murder? That can't be," he protested out loud. "I was here all fucking night," he affirmed as Detective White smiled and calmly strolled away from him, towards the door.

"Is that so?" she turned back and murmured to the room. "Then you better hope that it's not your 'unknown' blood all over the crime scene," she coyly whispered to herself but loud enough for him to hear.

"My blood?" was his loud and thunderous retort.

"Yes!" She replied with even greater contempt. She paused and took stock of the band-aide on his hand. The lab just confirmed it a few minutes ago. She was of course bluffing, wanting to see his response.

Bill was speechless, utterly bewildered, he froze in place. In the court of popular opinion, he was guilty as charged.

"I thought so," replied Detective White. "Let me guess," as she gazed at the wrapped bandage on his hand. "You cut your hand shaving and THAT will explain how so much of your blood is all over the room?"

Bill didn't answer, trying to recall where he had washed his hands after cutting himself on the Martini glass. "The guest bathroom," he remembered, "I was nowhere near the bedroom. How did this happen?"

The nurses leered at him in disgust. What little sympathy they had for him evaporated, even from Brenda.

"This wouldn't be a good time to leave town Doc," said Detective White. "I am sure I'll be paying you a visit in the very near future. And could you also stop by the lab soon? We need some blood sample from you for comparison sake that is." With that, she nodded to Detective Afoot and the other uni-formed personnel present as they exited the ICU with instruction to keep a sharp eye on Bill and for God's sake, do not allow the coward to finish what he wasn't man enough to do last night.

They made their way to the elevator. While waiting, Detective White de-cided to return for one more question. She made her way to Kelly's cubicle. She looked in, came out and headed straight to the Nurses Station. She looked around in bewilderment, as the good doctor was nowhere to be seen. "Has anyone seen Dr. Presser?" she asked.

"The lounge," gestured Brenda. Detective White continued to the back. She scanned the lounge, empty. She proceeded to the bathroom, equally empty.

"Shit!" She thought.

She returned to the front desk and asked, "Is there another way out of the ICU?"

Without looking up, Brenda pointed to the sign marked 'Emergency Exit' located in the back of the ICU.

She barely caught sight of Bill, as he exited. By the time she reached the door, the stairwell was ghostly silent.

Bill had intended on leaving the hospital; however, he remembered the multitude of pages he had received while in bed and the ICU and decided to exit on the second floor, find a phone, and answer them. He assumed they were from Vicky. "Had she? Impossible," he thought, "the timeline. Did she follow me home and hurt Kelly, then made her way back here? That's how she knew where to find me and fuck my brains out? How long after I left home was Kelly assaulted? No! No! Not enough time," he thought. "So when? Shit!" Bill felt nauseated by the aforementioned thoughts and leaned over the railing and heaved, but nothing came out. He gathered himself. He thought about going directly to the call room; instead, he exited one floor below and located a phone.

# Chapter 7

Vicky, asleep in her call room, was stirred from her slumber by noises she did not immediately recognize; clanging sounds outside the room. She sat straight up, knocking over the phone she had left in the bed.

She scanned the room for some sense of normalcy. "I hate these fucking moments," she thought as she recounted the numerous times she had awakened in a strange place, not having the faintest idea where she was. Falling asleep in different places at various hospitals and hotels will do that to you sometimes.

"Hospital! Ah yes!" Her head slowly cleared.

She now realized that she'd fallen asleep in the call room, waiting for Bill.

He never called and never showed up.

She glanced at the clock, 05:58.

A lot of things started coming back to her; the events of the prior day and night started to stream back to her consciousness, beginning with her case that went awry, the rain, Bill, her Nightingale Cap and of course, their lovemaking the night before. It all culminated with his absence from this cold bed, again! "I last left him in the OR, somewhere around 10pm. I came back here, crashed after I called and paged that asshole incessantly. I slept soundly though until now."

She bent over and located the phone on the floor. She leaned over, picked it up, paged him again, replaced it in the cradle, and returned the whole thing to its usual and customary place on the nightstand.

It rang almost immediately, before she even had a chance to let it go.

Surprised, she picked it up and spoke with an incredulous tone.

"Now that's a first," she said into the receiver.

"This is Detective White," she heard from the other end of the phone.

"Detective?" she thought.

"To whom am I speaking?"

"Oh! I'm sorry," she replied. "This is Vicky, I'm a Nurse Anesthetist with…"

"I know whom you are ma'am," Detective White dryly interjected. She and Vicky shared the same boyfriend a while back. Vicky remembered her as Nancy.

Detective Simpson left her for Vicky who in turn dumped him for Bill. Detective Simpson never recovered from that. Detective White should know; she hadn't stopped trying to regain his favor but he hadn't stopped pining for Vicky.

Surprised, Vicky freely responded, "I just paged Dr. Presser. I thought it was him calling back," she said. Sensing she was babbling, Vicky caught herself and quieted immediately. "What can I do for you," she said in a more serious tone, "Detective…?"

"White," was the short, curt reply. "So, are you saying that he is not with you and you haven't seen him?"

"DUH!" She thought, but answered that he was not. She rolled her eyes.

"Do you know of his whereabouts since last evening, after he left the OR?"

Bewildered by the line of questions, Vicky angrily responded, "If I knew, I would have called him directly or better yet, I would just roll over and talk to him instead don't you think? Wouldn't I?"

Exasperated, Vicky added, "I left him in the OR late last night and I haven't seen him since. Is everything OK?" she asked.

"Ma'am, are you aware of the events at his house last evening?"

Silence.

"Weird," Vicky thought. "Should I be impressed by the gossips of the Presser's household?" she quipped.

"There was an attack on Mrs. Presser last night," Detective White interjected.

Stunned, "No! No! I had no idea. When?" Vicky stymied over her words.

"Like I said. Last night," was the staunch reply. "Can you account for your times since the time you left the operating room last evening to now?"

"I was here," she said.

"Alone?"

"Yes, I was alone," she responded much more forcefully then she had intended, unsure of the ramification.

More silence.

"Ma'am, I am well aware that you were seen with Dr. Presser last evening. It won't take much for us to corroborate the timeline."

Vicky, still unsure of her next move, sounded fidgety over the phone. Although Detective White peppered her with a multitude of questions, the one that resonated was the one she wanted but didn't have an answer to: where the hell was Bill?

"He was not here—should I again reaffirm that?" she thought. Her mind drifted. He did say that he would 'take care' of Kelly. "Not what I had in mind, but, would it be wrong of me to derive pleasure from her demise? Whoa, is she even dead? She said attacked! What Happened? Yes! Attacked she said. The bitch was not dead." The thoughts, neither good nor bad, sickened her as Detective White wrestled her back to reality.

"Your affair with Bill is no secret," she said.

More silence, quite the dramatic pause.

"Can you tell me when was the last time you actually saw Dr. Presser?"

That was an easy one. She recounted seeing him in the OR and offered her help and so on.

She again drifted back to his words, "I'll take care of her!"

Vicky found and activated the hold button on her pager. "Beep, Beep, Beep," was the sound that reverberated from it.

"I have to get that," Vicky said. "Can you hold on?"

Before Detective White could protest, Vicky dropped the phone on the bed and withdrew to the back of the room. She fumbled for her cell phone and tried Bill again, but there was no answer.

"Time to compose myself," she thought.

She managed a smile as she thought of the number of times that the self-activating button on her pager had gotten her out of a messy jam.

"The benefits of being in the profession," she thought. Faking a page allowed her enough time to gather herself and ponder her next move. She wished Bill had answered her.

"Where the hell is he? I don't know what the fuck to do!" she mumbled as she pounded the bathroom counter with her open hand as she stared at her reflection in the mirror.

She took several deep breaths and returned to the phone and carried on with Detective White.

"So sorry Detective, can we take this up another time?"

"You have to go?"

"DUH!" was her thought, but the retort was, "Sorry, they need me in surgery; a G.S.W., (gun shot wound) to the chest just rolled in." She immediately regretted those words, as it would be very easy to verify later that this was a bold ass lie on her part, but she needed to end this conversation with the detective.

"I need you to stop by the station when you are done, or would you rather that I come to the OR? I'm in the hospital as we speak."

"Sure, sure, no, I mean no; I'll come to you."

"What would be a good time for you?"

"When you're done; I'm heading to the station now. I should be there for a while."

"Ok."

Detective White gave Vicky her compliment of numbers and an admonition to stay in touch and not to talk to anyone else in the meantime.

She hung up the phone and her thoughts were immediately disrupted by a set of raps on the door.

She ran and yanked opened the door.

"Bill, Thank God!" She stood frozen as his look of despair befell her. "Have you heard? Kelly, uh, she was..."

"Yes, yes," he said interruptedly. "I just left her bedside. Can you believe that they actually think I had something to do with it?"

Repulsed, Vicky replied, "I just found out myself too; a detective just called me. I didn't know quite what to say. I faked a page and got off the phone. I've been calling you. She asked me about you, us, last night. She made it sound like you were somehow involved Bill! Is that possible?"

"You know better than that!" was his fiery reply.

"Where the hell have you been? All night, where on God's earth could you have been not to answer me, Bill?"

"You don't want to know—trust me."

"Sigh!" Seeing the look on her face, Bill felt the need to speak out.

"I didn't do it Vicky! You know that," he said sternly. "I can't believe the stuff they are accusing me of," he blurted.

"I want to believe you Bill," were the words that regrettably came from Vicky. She desperately wanted to take them back but it was too late. She cringed at the thought of Bill wanting to strangle her for that last remark. He was not close enough to her but she could imagine the feel of his gigantic hands tightly wrapping around her throat, squeezing hard.

"The cat's out of the bag," she thought. "I might as well continue."

"They said that she was attacked some time after I last saw you Bill. She said that your blood type was recovered from the crime scene. They couldn't find you for hours."

"Your point is WHAT?"

"What am I supposed to think, Bill?"

Silence, as their body languages betrayed their respective positions on this.

"Well, it sounded like Detective White was trying to find out if you were really here with me or not. But, we BOTH know the answer to that question, don't we Bill? Where were you baby?"

She went on and berated him for fucking her and leaving her wanting more; for not coming back to her; for being the asshole that he is—she unloaded everything she never got a chance to tell him before.

More silence.

"You didn't come back here Bill. Where the hell were you? Where did you go? Home? Is that it Bill? It doesn't look good Bill!"

Perturbed, Bill slammed the door on his way out, which echoed loudly in her ears.

She equally responded by slamming her hands on the door as she fell to her knees, sobbing, not sure if it was for herself, Kelly, or worse, for Bill.

A good cry and some choice words later, Vicky dressed and threw on a hat and sunglasses she'd always kept in her bag for days like this.

She checked herself in the mirror. Satisfied that this was as good as it was going to get, she scanned the room and gathered her stuff and left.

# Chapter 8

Vicky made her way out of the call-room, down the hallway to the elevator. She thought about checking the operating room for the day's schedule and thought better of it—why bother? Instead, she returned to the room, called in and called-off for the day; she was too distraught to work.

She made her way back to the elevator, pushed the down button and waited.

"I'll fix him," she thought. "I will tell it all!"

The elevator door opened and the car was empty. She entered and pushed the button to the parking level. She searched her bag and retrieved the card with Detective White's phone numbers and clutched it to her chest, contemplating her next move.

Surprisingly, she made it all the way to the ground floor without stopping; it was still early morning at the hospital. During the day, the stairs would usually be much faster than the elevators, even to the top floors.

She located a phone behind the information desk in the lobby and dialed one of the numbers listed.

There were four rings.

"White here!"

"Oh! Hi. I didn't expect you to answer."

"You reached me on my cell phone."

"Makes sense; this is Vicky, Vicky from the hospital. Are you ready for me now?"

"Ok."

"I'm leaving the hospital now and should be there in about 20 minutes. Is that ok?"

"I'll be there in 10," White said.

"Then I'll see you soon. Bye," she said and hung up.

"What am I doing?" She reflected to herself. "That fucker can't go on treating me this way. And besides, I would only be telling the truth; right? No harm done if he's innocent," she thought. "If not, then I'll decide later how badly I want to lie for him."

With a smirk, Vicky checked her mirror image in the glass door, gathered herself, and exited the hospital.

She left the building via the main walkway, past the garden she frequented on so many occasions. Jasmines, her favorite, were in full bloom. She picked a bunch, inhaled them, and headed for the parking lot, still unsure of her actual destination—home or Detective White's office.

She reached the guard shack and waved to Frank, the night security guy who, as usual, was sound asleep and didn't stir until she rapped on the windowpane.

Frank stirred to life, startled by Vicky's giggles.

"Wanna ride to your car Ms. Vicky?" said Frank, as he got up from his chair and shamelessly tucked his shirttails into his pants.

Frank approached her, all the while, grinning as he motioned her to his four-seater EZGO golf cart fully equipped with air conditioner and XM satellite radio.

Giving her a ride would undoubtedly be one of, if not thee highlight of his day. As far as action goes around here, Frank hasn't seen any since the last car break-in almost three years ago when he surely was more spry and up to the task at hand. Nowadays, his presence is more symbolic than required.

Funny, she thought, Frank was almost 70, frail and always half asleep when she saw him. Who on God's Earth can he protect?

"No Thanks Frank. I can manage just fine," she added.

She continued around the bend, up the back stairwell towards her car. His eyes trailed her derrière as she disappeared and he halfway hoped that she would return, having changed her mind about the ride—she didn't. Frank sat down and resumed his slumber.

Vicky entered the stairwell and straightened her sweater; it tangled in her night bag as she tried to keep from squishing the bunch of Jasmines in her hand.

She could still smell Bill on her, somewhat clashing with the fresh flower buds; that drew a half smile, then despair.

She soon lost herself in her actions of the previous night. She was aroused, yet disappointed that Bill did not return to her. She had indeed checked the OR after talking to Detective White. He was done somewhere around midnight. *Give or take another 30 minutes for paper work and his ass should have been back in my arms—where he belonged.*

She was so distracted, so lost in her reverie, that she never heard the footsteps closing in on her, as she was about to emerge from the stairwell on the second floor. When she finally realized that she might not be alone, she quickly fumbled through her purse for her keys and the canister of pepper spray that she'd kept in her purse for the past five years, hoping she'd never need it.

Today, right now, she felt the need for it.

"Had I removed it? Was it any good?" All sorts of thoughts flashed through her head.

She could still hear her ex-boyfriend, the cop, telling her "Vicky boo, if you fail to prepare, you must be prepared to fail."

She found it. She was more prepared then she could have imagined. She could taste the sudden surge of adrenalin in her throat as she gathered herself. Almost to the exit, she hastened her pace.

"A couple more steps and I'll be out of the stairwell. Then, a hop and a skip to my car."She never made it. Vicky was always keenly aware of her diminutive stature, the frailty it exuded. "Hopefully, this idiot is no different," she thought. "I hope he underestimated me, just like the rest. I'll kick the shit out of him before he can realize that I am a trained martial art expert."

She was indeed prepared to take full advantage of his miscalculations. Whoever it was behind her, failed to read the same book she was reading. He grabbed her ponytail with such force that she felt every fiber on her hair loosen from her scalp. The force knocked her back on her ass.

She never trained for that maneuver in her martial arts classes. She was too startled to scream, but something must have registered as Frank woke up with the faint sound of someone in distress; he stirred to life but never responded.

She flailed at her attacker with all her might. By the time she regained her composure, he had her swathed in a hospital bedcover adorned with its infamous logo. She frantically kicked and swung her arms in an effort to get away. She made contact with his kneecap. His legs buckled. He grunted and dropped her like a sack of potatoes. Still swathed in the bedcover, she managed to barely roll out of the stairwell and unto the garage floor.

Seemingly pissed off, he caught up to her before she could unbundle herself and kicked her about her head until she stopped moving, then twice more for good measure.

Aware of all the camera angles, he pulled her back into the stairwell and quickly bounded her mouth, arms and legs with the duct tape he brought along.

When he was done, he methodically cleaned up the scene of all evidence of an altercation, including her purse and its strewed contents and of course, her pepper spray. He retrieved her car keys and the scattered Jasmines. He once again checked the garage for any sign of movement; there was nothing.

He dragged her body to her car via a circuitous path around several cars and pillars to avoid the rest of the cameras, all the while avoiding an upward gaze towards them just in case anyone, let alone Frank, was watching.

He then pulled out her keys from his pocket, pushed the button, and opened the trunk. The wailing sounds of her alarm horn and the simultaneous flashing of all of the car's lights immediately greeted him.

"Shit!" He recognized, too late, that he activated the panic mode rather than the trunk release button. To his muse, he realized that he had pushed the button that corresponded to the 'trunk release button' on his own car's remote control.

He quickly cancelled the panic mode and hid behind the car, waiting for a response, but nothing happened at this hour.

Vicky spurred to life and he quickly muffled her with a free hand. When that wasn't enough, he punched her across the face several times into submission.

All the while, he silently berated himself, again, for yet another amateurish act on his part.

"I've botched this all up," he thought. "How many more mistakes can I get away with? How long before the police close in on me? I'm taking care of their star witness," he thought.

That brought a smile to his otherwise clenched jaw.

He also realized that it had been some time since he had silenced the alarm. Aside from the occasionally random car passing by, no one had truly responded to all of that noise he made.

That was good.

"Let's get on with this," he whispered in her ears.

Still fighting about, she yelled, through the gag, what sounded like "Fuck you and your mother—that bitch you came from!"

"You," he shouted back, "of all people are the whore. You have the nerve to call someone a bitch? After that show you put on in the call room last night? That was very impressive. If I didn't know any better I would have sworn that you enjoyed yourself. Did you have a great time darling?"

He bent down and whispered some more sweet nothings in her ears while he fondled her breasts underneath the bedcover.

He enjoyed her firm glands and almost lost himself in the moment. Her muffled scream and body movements made him realize that he had her in a death grip; she was all contorted behind her car but he needed to get on with the task at hand.

He sighed and released her and she fell hard to the ground. "Calm down!" He instructed himself.

He responded to himself and again reached for the remote control. He made sure this time that he pressed the right button. He bent down and picked her off of the floor and shoved her in the trunk. She grunted as her head impacted against the back of her trunk.

"I'm sorry honey." Did I hurt you?" He said in playful mode.

He reached over and in a loving and gentle manner, caressed her hair, face, and neck. He paused awhile to identify the cricoid and then the thyroid cartilage just below the jaw line. He felt for her coratid artery on the side of her neck, just lateral to her trachea. Each rapid heartbeat pulsated so strongly that he could feel the flow of blood, gushing out of the left ventricle, through the aortic valve into the aorta as it coursed upward via the carotid artery and into the brain. He could almost feel each oxygen molecule making its way to its destination and feeding each and every brain cell that could not survive longer than four minutes without its elixir of life; a point he planned on testing soon, really soon.

Both of their heartbeats raced at a mile a minute; his would go on but hers would be extinguished any minute now.

"What a waste," he thought, "such a great piece of ass she could have been."

Then, with a swift and deliberate motion, he reached in his pocket and brandished a shiny scalpel with a brand new, unused 15 blade and slit her throat from ear to ear, starting from the right side of her neck and on to the left side. Vicky's body shook violently as blood, under extremely high-pressure from all the adrenalin coursing through her arteries, ricocheted off of everything within the confines of the trunk, his chest, and face. Undeterred, he held on as her body became more and more slippery from the spurting blood. The blade transitioned from skin, fat, connective tissues, and muscles, and transected both carotid arteries and jugular veins along with their respective tributaries. As vital as these vessels were to life, Vicky's preoccupation was with the vast network of nerve fibers transmitting excruciating pain to her brain. Normally great at multitasking, extreme pain had a way of harnessing all of the brain's processing powers and leave an indelible impression on the consciousness. Alone, there was no greater sensation than this level of pain or imminent death. Vicky was experiencing both simultaneously. When he reached the denser characteristic of the trachea with the blade, he dug deeper and severed it. Her body jerked more intensely and danced to no particular music while blood bubbles spewed from her neck not unlike the erupting lava shows seen emanating from Hawaii's Kilauea Volcano.

He held her down until her movements slowed to a stop. There were a few reflexive jerks that startled him so he held on until they too eventually stopped.

What seemed like an eternity later, the blood finally stopped spurting out of the arteries in her neck and simply oozed down her body, propelled only by gravity. All that remained were tiny blood bubbles, reminiscent of a warm mud bath he experienced a while back at a retreat in Northern California, and a slow ooze from the severed veins and muscles of her neck.

Her breath fell silent and her body slumped over in his arms. The smell of fresh, warm blood as it mixed with the muggy July air reminded him of the putrid slaughterhouses of yesteryears on the farm where he grew up.

All that could be heard was a constant drip of blood from beneath the trunk onto the garage pavement and the distant hustle and bustle of a new day dawning.

He stood up and felt her warm blood dripping down his face, down in his scrub shirt onto his chest. At first he thought it was perspiration, but this felt much, much warmer and thicker than sweat. He resisted the urge to taste her blood and instead massaged it, like some kind of rejuvenating cream, into every pore of his face.

He was so engrossed with the task at hand that he was unaware of how much time had actually elapsed.

Regaining his composure, he hurriedly got to his feet and scanned the garage; again, there was nothing.

He methodically went about cleaning up the scene in a hurried pace, not caring whether it was all cleaned up or not. He simply wanted to ensure that a large pool of blood would not attract anyone from a distance. Satisfied, he changed out of his blood soaked scrub suit into a fresh set and placed it with the rest of the items that came in contact with her into a plastic bag and set it aside in the trunk. He picked up the scalpel, stared at it, and made a mental note to change the blade before he used it again. He carefully replaced it with the rest of the surgical instruments he had earlier wrapped and was now so accustomed to carrying with him. He wiped the outside of the trunk, the remote control, her keys, and as much of the floor behind the car as he could. To the untrained observer, nothing was grossly afoul.

Again satisfied, he gathered the plastic bag and was startled by the blue sedan that pulled into the stall three cars removed.

He quickly ducked behind the rows of cars on the other side and made his way toward the stairwell, well out of camera's view. The last glimpse he took of the crime scene froze him in place.

"YOU FUCKING IDIOT!" he mumbled to himself.

Her driver side door was left opened for all to see.

He contemplated going back, but instead, realized that it was probably for the best that she would be discovered sooner rather than later.

With that, he continued down the stairs onto the ground floor.

As expected, Frank was sound asleep. He was able to evade the last of the cameras as he made his way toward the side streets, into his truck and unto the morning traffic.

Although her car remained in the lot with the driver side door opened, her body was not discovered until midday.

By then, as Detective White knew from the surveillance videos, Bill had left the hospital shortly before Vicky had earlier this morning; his current location was still unknown.

It took a while longer for the crime lab analysis to reveal that the blood in the trunk was, as anticipated, type A+ which was Vicky's, and to everyone's surprise, Type O- which was the same as Bill's, and unexpectedly, a small quantity of Type B-, source unknown.

# Chapter 9

Earlier, Bill angrily stormed away from Vicky and returned to his own call room, changed into a fresh set of scrubs, made his way back to the operating room, and scanned the day's schedule. "I must carry on as if this is a normal day," he thought. "Everyone thinks I'm guilty. Fuck!"

Unable to focus, he finally admitted to himself that he could not function in a safe manner, located the charge nurse, and informed her that he was leaving. Perplexed that he had even reported for duty, she promised him that she would fix the schedule and that he should go home and regroup.

He thanked her, no small feat for Bill, and he exited. Bill returned to the call room but to his chagrin, Vicky had already departed.

He left and headed for the ICU again. Halfway there he thought better of it and diverted to the cafeteria for a cup of coffee. His mind raced, analyzing the predicament he found himself in. He wandered about in a daze and again thought of Vicky and Kelly. He made his way down the back stairs, out of the building to his car, and eventually decided to leave the compound all together. He looked about his car, located his cell phone, and called the OR and was told that Vicky took the day off.

"Shit!" he thought.

He called her cell and the call immediately went to voice mail. "Is it bad reception or was she avoiding me? I need to talk to her," he thought.

In no time, he made his way across town to her town house, not knowing if she'd even want to talk to him after the way they parted earlier.

Nothing of last night made sense to him.

"How can my life unravel so quickly?" he thought.

He mindlessly continued to her house, turned the corner, and was surprised to see several uniform cars at her place.

"What the fuck?"

He was too close to the scene by then to turn around and he tried to slowly pass the cacophony of traffic about her place. Unfortunately, his car was easily recognized and a uniform officer pointed to him and all hell broke loose thereafter. Before long, they were in a full on pursuit down the back streets of Fresno. He tried to outrun the black and whites but unfortunately the busy morning traffic impeded his progress. With ample back up, he was easily cornered at gunpoint and was apprehended in full view of the overhead news helicopters and the many eye level cameras recording his attempted flight from the law.

He resisted and by the grace of god, was not killed in the ensuing struggle.

Bill was aggressively subdued, handcuffed and placed in the back of a car, all the while protesting his innocence.

Everything churned in slow motion as he stared into a camera that was recording his every emotional contortion. Bill was on national television as he sat in the back of the cruiser, head slumped down, looking ever like the guilty perp caught in action.

The scene calmed down and Bill was taken to the station as a deflated man. The trip to nowhere was surreal. The buildings, streets, and traffic whizzed by in a blur as his mind raced at warped speed, trying to make sense of the events of the last 24 hours. This was way wrong he thought. Kelly was brutally attacked, and she now lay in a bed at his and her hospital, dying and he couldn't help her. "I'm supposed to protect her and I have failed miserably," he thought.

He envisioned the news cycle reporting his guilt and had no idea how he got here, let alone how he would get out of this.

What a whirlwind day this was, Bill thought. He went from a hero to a zero in a matter of a day. He'd had all the time to come to grips with being in a holding cell no larger than a standard department store's hallway bathroom for the brutal attack on his wife and he still couldn't make sense out of it. Now, almost 10 PM, he remained perplexed as to why this was happening to him.

"What next?" he thought, seemingly unaware of the events that transpired since he left the hospital 18 hours ago.

He managed to cajole a sympathetic detective to let him use the phone again and he called the hospital to check up on Kelly. Nurse Eileen sternly told him to never call here again and forcefully hung up the phone, which loudly reverberated in his ear. He was persistent and after many more tries, he reached the back table and talked to Brenda who reluctantly filled him in on Kelly's failing condition. He tried Vicky and again got her answering service on the first ring. Frustrated, he reached his attorney at home and filled him in on the events of the day. To his surprise, his attorney was all too aware of the events as he was reported as the leading news story in a usually quiet town. He promised Bill that he would see him in a few hours, as soon as he concluded an important manuscript.

"Talk to no one," was the final admonition from his attorney.

Bill was so angry at the response that he slammed the phone against the wall, smashing it into pieces. "Fuck you!" He said out loud. "I pay you well enough not to be second fucking fiddle to anyone," he added even more forcefully.

Not a smart move with 'Bubba' somewhat patiently waiting his turn to use the phone.

In no time, Bill was pinned against the wall with a giant size fist heading his way.

"What's the matter," said Bubba. "You got something against defenseless women and phones sweet cake?"

Before Bill could muster up an answer, the uniforms were all over Bubba with nightsticks and fists.

For his own safety, Bill was whisked away into an entirely different part of the precinct.

Bill gathered himself and when he finally settled down, all he could think of was how disfigured Kelly looked, the empty pain in her eyes. "How can anyone think that I had anything to do with it?" All other thoughts ceased at that time, as the events of the past few days befell upon him. Bill felt numb.

Somehow, Bill found himself in full recall mode. He reminisced about the very first time he laid eyes on Kelly; much different than the way she looked earlier. That brought a wry smile to his tired face, no different than every other times that he'd thought of her, albeit lately, after only a few drinks.

As a young intern, Bill was known as an intense clinician and an even more extreme skirt chaser. He was always on the prowl. He had an insatiable appetite for the young and unsuspecting nursing students.

Kelly was different; she caught him off guard. He usually had a lead on all of the new, pretty, and desirable conquests at the hospital. So on this particular day, when he arrived at the ICU and caught sight of Kelly, he was caught of-fkilter and his heart literally skipped a beat.

She was indescribably beautiful. Her long and wavy dark hair marched to a different beat from her alternately bouncing voluptuous breasts as she walked; they were barely confined within her candy striper uniform.

Her every movement seemed to occur at a step slower than slow while his heart pulsed in double time. She must have sensed his penetrating stare, so much so that she made a full turn toward the door and him. Unfazed, he smiled at her and clearly mouthed, "A woman in uniform!"

She blushed, yet stayed composed. She then smiled and continued around the corner, soon to be out of sight.

Bill hurriedly pushed the patient that he was transporting to the ICU into a cubicle and chased after Kelly. In the process, he knocked over an IV pole loaded with a bottle of Nitroglycerin; glass chards flew everywhere. The noise, in an otherwise quiet ICU was deafening.

The patient clutched her chest and turned several shades of blue.

Fortunately, Bill had another bottle in the bed; always the paranoid type, he'd always devised a 'worst-case scenario' plan and this was as bad as it could get.

Pissed off Vicky, then his instructor in Anesthesia, located the new bottle in the bed, hung it, and in no small feat, managed to stabilize the patient. Hell was to be paid for his latest transgression; she was growing weary of his antics and something had got to give soon or a patient will irreparably be harmed.

Bill eventually caught up to Kelly and for the first time in his life, Bill was speechless. Having regained the upper hand, she dismissed his awkward advances all in plain sight of all and disappeared into the nursing lounge.

"She loves me," was all he could muster up to Brenda as she witnessed the whole exchange from the vintage point at the nursing station. Pathetically, Bill grinned from ear to ear as he patted his chest, feigning love pain or simple palpitations.

Phone in hand, Brenda was ready to report him. But, that wretched look on his face changed her mind. Love was in the air allright, but it was he who was a bit smitten.

Weeks followed and Bill was no closer than that first encounter. His every move and invitation was met with an unmistakable rejection. "She smiled at me the first time our eyes met," he confessed to Brenda one day. "Why does she hide any sign of interest?"

"Maybe it's your reputation that scares her, young Dr. Presser," replied Brenda.

"She needs to be convinced that you are sincere."

It clicked.

The next day, he waited for her by her car with a single rose in hand.

She slowed her gait as she caught sight of him but did not retreat. He waited as she neared him, enjoying her gait. "Remember this day," he confidently proclaimed out loud, as she reluctantly approached.

"This day," he continued, "we will tell our grandchildren, all twelve of them, was the day when grandma fell madly in love with grandpa."

He bowed and offered her the rose.

She blushed and gleefully accepted it. For a moment, she, still in her uniform wondered how he knew which car was hers. "Of course he knew," she relented, "he's the famous Dr. Presser, the magician."

They spoke uninterruptedly for hours. The sun went down and the air chilled before they both took stock of the time.

She reluctantly got into her car and drove away. The smile on her face said it all. She was his for the taking.

From then on, they were inseparable. For the first time in his life, Bill heeded his heart and not his genitals. Everyone took stock of the new Bill. He floated to the OR, the ICU, the ER, and on rounds—everywhere he went. He was a changed man. He greeted each day with her likeness and faded to black each night with the specter of seeing her again the next day.

He sent flowers to the ICU, her house, and her mother's house every Friday like clockwork until she finally pleaded that he stopped. He posted love notes on the main board in the lounge and on her car windshield. He played love songs on her answering service. He told all within ear shout how infatuated he was. It was easy. He truly meant it.

He remembered calling every day and how they chatted for hours on end when they couldn't see each other.

This was not exactly what he had bargained for, but he had to admit, he loved every minute of it.

This must be what has been missing in his life all along. She was different. They were married a year to the date from the parking lot scene.

Sharp raps on and a rapid swing of the door interrupted Bill's latest trek through yesteryears. He gathered himself, waited, and eventually, the scene was set.

The look on Detective White's face was indicative of the news to follow. Several others who he did not recognize but knew that they wouldn't be his advocates followed her entrance.

She began by outlining the sequence of events of the day starting with when he left the OR after the code with Mrs. Ryan. She continued through him leaving and returning for the surgery on Mrs. Robinson.

She made no mention of the interlude with Vicky in the call room. "Does she know?" he wondered.

Additionally, Detective White made a point to omit Vicky's gruesome attack earlier that morning. She wanted to hear what Bill would offer as an alibi for that timeline.

Even Bill had to admit that there were many inconsistencies with his whereabouts that day. He wanted to fill in the blanks but realized how sleazy that would sound, him fucking Vicky around the time of Kelly's attack, and he decided to keep silent. He sensed that Detective White was sympathetic to him but remembered the old mantra: 'Say nothing to the Police.'

He remained quiet and closed his eyes.

He wanted to evoke his right to counsel but "I have nothing to hide," was his thought and he forged on.

He protested his innocence quite profusely and deep down felt that Deective White wanted to believe him at the very least but her animosity seemed misplaced.

She observed him and waited for his next move, buying time. He knew that trick and ignored all as his head slumped down to his chest, almost falling asleep to the casual observer.

Deep down, she herself had issues with the narratives of the case so far. There was the matter of the preliminary report on the blood collected at both crime scenes. Other than that, there were no real physical findings placing Bill at both scenes. The time line also seemed a little too tidy to her. This would have had to be a well planned and timed double homicide, all the while keeping up with his surgery schedule, or two single unrelated events carried out by two separate perps for that matter. "How likely can both scenarios be?" she asked herself.

Other than the unexplained cut on his hand, Bill had no other physical signs of an altercation. He seemed quite composed for a man having gruesomely attacked two people he professed to love in one form or another. Both settings concerned her. He's either a calculated cold-blooded killer or an innocent man. The former chilled her that there might be more bodies to come as she was dealing with a serial killer right in front of her. Or, a similarly descriptive person is out there on the loose and is trying to frame Dr. Presser.

She was not sure which narrative scared her the most but a bird in hand...

She decided to play it conservatively and was now in search of excuses to bind him over until she could sort out the details and have a conclusive and final result from the crime lab on all the blood and DNA materials collected. Bill, however, being no stranger to a holding cell, tried to play it cool and pretend that he did not pick up on her tactics. Feigning sleep, he recalled the first time he was arrested for what he referred to as a simple misunderstanding. As a medical student at the U in San Diego, Bill was accused and arrested for having sex with an underage girl, the daughter of the then Dean of the School of Medicine, to be exact. He was taken in and grilled incessantly even as he protested his innocence and his repeated request for counsel was denied. They had him dead to right and thought they could break him and garnish a confession. They couldn't.

This was personal. The young Bill Presser had a penchant for younger girls, a point well known to the local police department. They finally had a reliable parent ballsy enough to press charges and they were hell bent on righting a long overdue wrong.

Bill's break came as the lead detective finally acquiesced and summoned his counsel who had him bailed out in no time. Bill, ever the showoff, immediately returned to the hospital, trying to carry on as normally as he could.

His luck took an even bigger turn for the best, as later that day he was assigned to a patient who presented to the Emergency Room with an apparent hot Appendix. The patient, a belligerent and gregarious man, could be heard in all parts of the ER. Bill cautiously approached the room and pulled back the curtain revealing a man in obvious discomfort.

"What the hell do you want?" was the immediate snarl.

Bill flashed his million-dollar smile, extended his hand, and introduced himself and promised to turn that frown into a smile if allowed five minutes to navigate through what seemed like a complex situation. He held the man's gaze and raised an eyebrow in a pleading gesture.

He swore the man almost let down his guard but he quickly recovered and retorted, "You're not old enough to change this bedpan, let alone fix me son! Now get the hell out of here and fetch me a real doctor."

Not easily swayed, the young Bill Presser forged on. "Au contraire my friend," he said, with a wry smile. "That's the problem here sir. All the real doctors are off tending to 'real serious' cases and consider you to be a low priority. Translation: they may not get to you for another 3 hours. That's where I come in. Again, give me five minutes and I'll make you believe that you can fix all that ails this world, the proverbial rose-colored glasses theory."

The man bit.

After a quick medical interview and physical exam, Bill excused himself with a promise to return with the cavalry.

Unsure what that entailed, the old man gritted his teeth and settled down in hope that this overzealous teenager could deliver on what he promised.

Bill made his way to the Med Room, looked about to make sure he was not spotted, punched in the code on the keypad on the wall and entered the restricted area. How he got the code was another story. Low-level employees, and Med Students were as far removed from restricted access areas as it got, and Bill by all accounts should not have been an exception. But Bill was different. By his 4th day on that rotation, Bill bedded the charge nurse, a cute and petite blond from South Africa and finessed all kinds of information, included the code to the med room out of her.

He was not sure at the time what he would do with that information but he figured it would come in handy one day. He had no interest in the contents of that room but the mere fact that it was restricted meant that he had to have that code.

Bill meandered through the room and collected an assortment of vials to mitigate his client's pain.

Bill sauntered back to the entrance, looked through the glass door. He was satisfied that the coast was still clear and exited as if he belonged there. Ever the natural thief, no one took notice.

Bill returned to his now new best friend and explained what was about to take place. Against all rules and regulations, Bill proceeded to medicate his patient over the next five minutes. The man was so comfortable, he could have pilfered every last secret out of him. The man turned out to be a pleasant, yet staunchly, but grateful individual once his pain was under control.

Thirty minutes later, as his patient's demeanor was polar opposite of the man who checked in an hour earlier, the ER attending Dr. Griswald, walked in requesting an update. Something was afoul he immediately observed.

This was supposed to be a patient in excruciating pain, yet this man was calm, smiling at him and expelling pleasantries.

He queried Bill for an explanation and Bill feigned his innocence.

Dr. Griswald stormed out of the room and confronted the charge nurse as to who medicated this patient against all protocols.

She, oblivious to Bill's interventions, loudly protested and resented the implication that she or a member of her staff was stupid enough to intervene.

Under normal circumstances, it was not ideal, actually it was dangerous to medicate a patient being evaluated for a serious condition, and in this case an Acute Appendicitis, until the diagnosis was clear. The best asset one had to direct the appropriate care was pain, which would have been very suggestive of a changing condition. But, it was completely taken away by the meds Bill gave him. Fortunately, the ER crew had already done the bulk of the work up, lab tests, and CAT scan and they were pretty confident that that man needed to go to the OR.

Otherwise, his improving pain status might have led them to conclude that he was getting better and discharged him with a simmering condition, masked by the pain meds that could have killed him if he did not return to the hospital in time.

Confused, Dr. Griswald reluctantly called the surgeon who eventually removed what was characterized as a severely inflamed Appendix. Any further delay would have required a more extensive colon resection and a 2-weeks+ hospitalization and umpteen potential complications as opposed to a 2-day, uneventful stay.

The next day, Bill visited that man who was completely unaware of the gravity of his interventions in the ER and he thanked Bill profusely for being the future of medicine, a caring physician who took the time to treat his patients as human beings rather than as corpses.

Fast-forward several weeks later now, after several motions by his attorney to dismiss the charges of statutory rape brought forth against him on the ground that his Miranda Rights were violated based on Bill's numerous requests for counsel prior to his interrogation, Bill was standing in open court, presided by his patient from the hospital.

Bill smirked.

Judge Spiller, that man, maintained his usual dour demeanor. He listened patiently over the next 30 minutes and surprisingly rendered an immediate decision. He summarily scolded the prosecutor and especially the detectives of record and promptly dismissed all charges on procedural grounds.

Bill floated out of the courtroom with everyone oblivious to how he managed to dodge these serious charges.

Thus began the legendary exploits of the young Bill Presser, the Midas King, The Comeback Kid, The Teflon Meister; he could not settle on a moniker for himself but he knew he was and would always be above the law. His charismatic demeanor would always find a way to rise above the fray. He feared no one; on that day, he declared himself, 'The Man,' supplanting Judge Spiller as the one who could do no wrong.

# Chapter 10

Earlier that day, Mrs. Robinson, who spent last night in the ICU unable to speak because of the breathing tube still lodged in her throat and connected to the ventilator, was now waking up and resting comfortably in a private room on the fourth floor, minus that awful machine.

As horrific and excruciating as the recollection of the pain of her surgery was last night, she cringed even more at the recall of her effort to breathe for the first 30 minutes post op. She recalled waking up on the table after loosing consciousness sometime after the horrific start of the surgery. Now off the ventilator, she was transported from the OR to the ICU and was being hand-ventilated by Dr. Presser with the aid of a small and portable Ambu Bag connected to the endotracheal tube. On more than one occasion she recalled, the asshole forgot to squeeze the Ambu bag and breathe for her and she was left to ponder when he would actually depress that bag and deliver her the much-needed oxygen molecules. She would wait for what seemed like an eternity, feeling the burn welling up in her chest, as she became more and more oxygen deprived. The ride was only a few minutes in length but she began to anticipate and crave the next breath from her master like a lifelong crack addict in search of a rock from her dealer. Bill, oblivious to all of this, parsimoniously delivered her much needed air when he seemed to recall that that was his only freaking obligation during the transport. She got madder and madder recalling his haphazard approach to her. In the ICU, the mechanical ventilator she was again connected to was the opposite. It was quite liberal with the air it dispensed whether she wanted or needed it or not. The machine would counter every effort she made. It would sometimes suck her breath out as she attempted to inhale but even worse, it would inflate her lungs after she'd taken a full deep breath, doubling her lung capacity, stretching every capillary and stitch in her abdomen. The pain searing through her was indescribable. At times, she felt every cell in her body scream in agony. She prayed for the machine to stop but it ignored her every plea. She tried to cry out but couldn't. She could not talk because of this tube wedged between her vocal cords, keeping them from fully opening and closing and allowing the anatomy of sound making. She also tried to move but couldn't. She felt restrained against an invisible rope that bound her from head to toe. She remembered Nurse Eileen alternating between looking and shining a flashlight into her eyes as if she was trying to extract every story she'd ever learned. Nurse Eileen seemed concerned that her pupils were not reacting as a patient that should have had residual anesthesia and sedation on board. Mrs. Robinson appeared to be wide-awake, but remained motionless in the bed. Eileen muttered that this was not possible unless... She shook off the thought and summoned her colleague who came over and evaluated Mrs. Robinson with the same grave concern. They both arrived at the same conclusion; she was much too awake for their liking. They quickly adjusted her infusion pumps and within 3 minutes, an eternity in her present condition, Mrs. Robinson quietly slipped into unconsciousness. As the shades came down over her eyes, she mercifully tumbled into a Midazolam and Fentanyl haze that was dripping in her through the IV line.

She woke up later, actually the next day, in this room breathing on her own without that monstrous machine and that awful tube in her throat. Her posterior pharynx was rubbed raw from the irritation caused by the tube but it was still far better than having that wretched thing still lodged between her vocal cords. She could now speak, albeit in a raspy voice, but she could talk nonetheless. She looked around and confirmed that she indeed was out of the ICU, in a different room, much quieter than the former.

As her head cleared, she surmised that she was in a regular floor room, thus accounting for the quietness.

She soon began to replay in her head the horror of the previous day. The TV was on and the attack on Kelly was front and center. She watched and began to piece it all together.

"I know what happened!" she screamed.

She let out a blood-curdling scream that summoned all available nurses and attendants to her room. The first to arrive was Marie Sue who was her assigned nurse. Mrs. Robinson was sobbing so uncontrollably that Mary Sue wanted to sedate her but Mrs. Robinson waved her off. She pointed to the TV, and the reporter who was retelling the story of that woman identified as Mrs. Presser who was brutally attacked recently. She was not making any sense through her tears and intermittent gasps. Then she finally heaved and said, "I know who did this," as she collapsed on the bed from exhaustion. Mrs. Robinson was quickly whisked back to the ICU for observation and monitoring.

When she woke up again, she was surrounded by a different set of staff including Dr. Williams who she clearly recalled tortured her incessantly in surgery. She began to sob again but this time she was immediately medicated just enough to dull the pain and the recall from the previous day. Dr. Williams approached her. He took her hands in his and in an apparent confusion, she stiffened up. She withdrew her hands several times before she allowed him to hold on to them. She wept softly and asked if that girl was still here and if she was still alive.

"Which girl," he inquired.

"Mrs. Presser," was the reply. "I know what, Eh! I know who did it. It was that monster Dr. Presser, her husband," she murmured as the tears freely rolled down her cheeks this time.

All in attendance grew eerily quiet, wondering how she could possibly know what they all suspected all along. They wanted her to continue but the medications finally caught up to her and she was soon fast asleep.

Concerned, they were all in agreement that they had to summon Detective White, who wanted to know the moment Kelly woke up and was able to talk. This seemed as close as it would get since Kelly was circling the drain by the minute. Her condition was deteriorating rapidly and no one was optimistic that she would ever recover. Kelly was battling a raging infection, sepsis, as it is known, that seemed to emanate from her abdominal cavity. No one could figure out how it was possible that she was so grossly contaminated with intestinal bacterial flora since her gut was intact from mouth to anus. How could she have this infection? What could possibly be the source? No one, save for her amateurish yet brilliant attacker, in hindsight, could comprehend that the extensive contamination in her abdominal cavity was from his stomach contents when he threw up all over her. Stomach contents were quite acidic and caustic to normal tissue outside the confinement of its usual surrounding. It was incomprehensible how quickly it could overwhelm even a normal healthy person let alone a person in Kelly's condition. It was not looking good for her.

Even though she is on a heavy regimen of broad-spectrum antibiotics, she had not responded to any of them. Her white blood cell count was steadily climbing and it was only a matter of time before the infection overpowered her and her internal organs would begin to fail, one at a time. She was now in God's hands.

Detective White arrived and had to wait another 15 minutes for the sedatives to wear off before she could interview Mrs. Robinson.

In the meantime, she paced about the nursing station, taking notice of the machinery of the ICU. Mrs. Robinson's room was set in a semicircle, almost directly across from Kelly's room. The two rooms, although physically similar in size and configuration, couldn't be anymore different. The action in Kelly's room was so active and fast paced with all the lights that she was never alone in the room; no wonder no one could actually get any rest in an ICU room. In contrast, Mrs. Robinson's room was eerily quiet, with the lights dimmed to minimum, inhabited by only one lonely orderly tending to her IV's. It was easy to tell which one probably would not survive the night. The nurses minding Mrs. Robinson opened her cubicle door to check in on her. That seemed to have startled the orderly who hurriedly left the room without speaking to either one of the nurses, almost bumping into Detective White as he exited. Astonished at his abruptness, Detective White looked at him then back at the nurses, who both shrugged. They faintly recognized him but could not pinpoint who he was. They took inventory of the room and nothing seemed out of line. They quizzed Mrs. Robinson who was now awake and equally perplexed as to the nature of that strange man in her room. Finding no further irregularities, the detective moved in for what turned out to be one of the most incredulous interviews she had ever conducted.

# Chapter 11

Bill's latest dreamscape through San Diego was interrupted by a series of loud conversations emanating from deep inside the precinct. He recognized one of the voices as none other than Greg Harding, Esq., his attorney of record. He smiled.

By the time Greg made his way to the interrogation room, Bill was on his feet with all of his personal belongings in his hands, ready to go home.

"Get me the hell out of here!" he charged Greg.

His hope of such a departure was dashed by the fact that: 1. These were serious charges and 2. This was a busy and embarrassing time within the department following several high profile screw-ups in the not so distant past that has made everyone cautious with early or premature releases.

The most notable transgression was one Alejandro Valdamar, a high ranking South American Diplomat, accused of mowing down a 14 year old innocent bystander while in what should have been a stuporous coma given his blood alcohol level. He was released to his embassy only to kill the local congressman's daughter under an eerily similar circumstance.

Much to their protest, and threat of motions and lawsuits, Bill was bound over for further questioning. Incredulously, Bill slumped back into his chair and allowed the heavyweights to carry on the conversation while he pouted. The dispute went on until they were both reminded that Bill fled from the police and put up quite a resistance earlier that morning; he might still have to face charges yet to be determined for the latter two events if the need arose.

Even with the particulars of the day, Detective White still entertained the idea of releasing him. She genuinely felt an attraction to, hatred towards, and sorrow for him but even more, she was troubled by the time line and was having trouble connecting him to all the events of the day. She had yet to mention Vicky's attack and Bill seemed to be only preoccupied with Kelly. "Is he involved with Vicky's death as well? If so," she thought, "he's sure playing it super cool." She must admit however, this wouldn't be the first time her gut instincts betrayed her and she decided to play a hunch.

She approached him with a coy demeanor and an added wry smile for show. She placed both hands on the table, directly in front of him and leaned forward. Gravity took over enough for her blouse to sag open, revealing her full breasts, almost down to her areola peaking over the edge of her lacy, mid cup bra. She smiled. She should cover up but she elected not to.

"Come on Bill," she said, "just tell us what really happened to Kelly that night. Tell us how she pissed you off and you snapped. We know all about your legendary temper; it is well documented Bill. I'm sure you didn't mean to gut her like that prized Marlin in your man-cave and..." Bill's eyes steeled, and he lunged at her; not what she had planned for.

Expecting an element of surprise from him, that is if he was really innocent, he should not know anything about the details of Kelly's brutal attack since they had yet to be made public.

Caught off guard she failed to respond in time as he wrapped both hands around her neck and squeezed.

Detective Afoot, a bit more cynical, anticipated Bill's response, given the accusatory tone of his partner, moved in to intercept Bill as quickly as he jumped out of his chair and caught Bill in mid stride. Bill's momentum and his sheer weight overwhelmed both detectives and all three of them crashed through the table. Bill, with both hands still firmly wrapped around Detective White's neck, his neck veins bulging out of his shirt, was determined to extinguish the life out of her for her ill-conceived accusations. He saw red and felt nothing short of the pain Kelly must be experiencing in that cold hospital bed. The two uniforms in the room were slow to respond. They finally sprang into action and made it to the collection of bodies that crashed through the interrogation table in 3 long strides; they did their best to separate the individuals and extract Bill's fingers from Detective White's throat.

Greg, unaccustomed to violence, even though he has represented a few of the seediest clowns in this town, shrank to the back of the room and waited.

Bill was still in great shape for his age and held his own albeit fueled by the rage of the image of Detective White's description of Kelly's attack. He mauled at anyone and anything within arm's reach. During the ensuing melee, Detective Afoot's left arm snapped loudly as he screamed even louder.

Greg tried to verbally intercede from afar. He tried in vain to calm Bill down; no such luck today. Reinforcement soon arrived and Bill was finally subdued and order was somewhat restored in the room.

Bill found himself face down with several big bodies restraining him. He could barely breathe and felt his every pulsating heart beat heaving through his chest. He was still enraged.

His thoughts were squarely on Kelly.

"How could this happen?" He thought.

Sensing futility, he eventually relaxed and allowed himself to be cuffed and rolled over onto his back. Order was reestablished in the room with everyone breathing heavily and straightening up as if they were preparing for a photo shoot. All were calm except Detective Afoot who still writhed on the floor in excruciating pain while clutching his obviously broken and disfigured arm.

Greg finally approached Bill with caution and admonished him to calm down and "Shut the Fuck Up!" All gains he had made towards his release were lost, he thought. There was no sense in sugarcoating this. There will be no liberation tonight or anytime soon for that matter, he informed Bill as much, but all of that fell on his death ears. Bill resumed his tirade, calling Detective White every foul name he could possibly recall, and he had an extensive vocabulary.

Greg begged of him to reconsider his predicament and ruminate on the consequence of his aforementioned actions.

Bill, still angry about Detective White's harsh tone, cowered but continued to glare at her as if he was still searching for an angle to resume his battery on her. She motioned to the two uniforms. They dragged Bill away as far as they could to the other side of the room and stood as a protective barrier between the two combatants.

When true order was restored, she approached Bill again, seemingly peering into his soul.

"Allow me to update you with some facts Big Boy!" said Detective White through flaring nostrils and clenched teeth. The dour look on her face foretold the grim reality facing Bill.

"I trust you remember who Mrs. Robinson is?" asked Detective White, pausing for effect.

"Rings a bell, but I'm sure you will refresh my memory," was the tired reply from Bill, as he hung his face into his mitten-sized hands.

"Mrs. Robinson was the lady you anesthetized the night in question, the night Kelly was attacked. The night you claim to have no real timeline for your actions."

Bill gave no response.

"Heads up Doc! She's not enamored with your bedside manners or your clinical skills for that matter. She intends on filing a complaint with the medical board as soon as she is released from the hospital. I'm sure you will hear about that real soon. I'm not here to do your bidding for you, but where I come in is that I just finished interviewing her in the hospital. Sorry Doc, that's what really kept us so long tonight. But guess what she said? She claims to have total recall of the whole surgical procedure. She remembered it all Doc, everything that was said and done during that procedure."

Detective White smiled and let the weight of that statement sink in as Bill slowly lifted his head and focused on Detective White, letting her words permeate through his consciousness.

"How do you surmise that can be Doc?" she continued.

For the first time, Bill's demeanor registered an element of fear and surprise, and for good measure. His analytical mind immediately accessed the night in question.

"Good God! It all makes sense now." he thought.

His conversation with Vicky was being played back with the added current events in mind.

Now he remembered that something did in fact bother him about that whole case and that evening but he was too distracted to put it all together. Now it was all coming back to him—all too clear.

"That bitch set me up! No! She wouldn't, she couldn't do that." He admitted to himself. "Is it possible? The call room; she'd never seduced me quite like that before," he thought.

"The syringes, Vicky's syringes, were out of sequence. I did not fill them. What on God's Earth did I inject? This is an anesthesiologist's worst nightmare (next to death of course)—a patient recalling everything that occurred in surgery. The conversations, the jokes and the comments they may have made about them seem meaningless and benign until now." Given his current predicament, that is of greater concern."

A million things flashed before him. They all merged to the same point. He was in deep shit!

"She set me up!" He said again. "That fucking bitch set me up!" He repeated. "She wouldn't, she couldn't possibly do that to me," he repeated, "why?" "You know why asshole," was his immediate retort, all to himself. Sometimes, Bill could be his own worst critic.

In truth, he thought, this was not about him; it was all about her, Vicky. With Kelly out of the way, he would have no more excuses not to be with her.

"But why frame me? I would be of no use to her from behind bars, on death row.

None of this makes any sense!" he thought as his mind raced to find a suitable answer.

Any doubt that Detective White had in her mind about Bill's guilt or innocence evaporated as Bill slumped, exasperated, into the chair and mouthed "Oh My GOD!" as he buried his face into his hands.

"THINK!" he said out loud, carrying on as if he was alone.

The sequence was clear. First and foremost, he fucked up in several ways:

1. Never, ever trust any syringes drawn by someone else—even *Mother Fucking Theresa* can make mistakes.

2. A patient recalling her surgery all the while he was telling his mistress how he would 'take care' of his wife who happened to be attacked several hours later or before—hours he cannot account for.

Once again, Bill thought, "How much worse can it get?"

Bill reverted to his earlier days of Anesthesia 101. Normally, the sequence of anesthetizing a patient was a very simple process. First, you would render the patient unconscious, essentially turning the brain off. This can be achieved within ten seconds with an injection of Pentothal, Propofol, or any combination of anesthetic agents. Once unconscious, the patient would stop breathing fifteen seconds later. The next step involves an injection of a paralytic agent to relax the face and neck muscles in order to intubate the patient, the process of placing an endotracheal tube into the trachea, the windpipe, for ventilating the lungs and thus, oxygenating the patient.

"Truth be known, my pet monkey can do this without a paralyzing agent, but it can certainly be more difficult without it," he thought.

Now that he thought about it, that night, the whole process seemed awkward, more strenuous than usual.

"She felt the whole damn thing!" he blurted out to no one. "Damn! What an ordeal it must have been," he admitted to himself.

He was distracted by Vicky and paid very little attention to the case. No one else was close enough to hear them, except for Mrs. Robinson.

The alarms on the anesthesia machine that night, resonated loudly again in Bill's head, just as they did the night in question. He recalled turning them all off shortly thereafter and normalizing her elevated blood pressure and heart rate soon after he anesthetized her as if they never mattered, as if nothing was wrong. In reality, nothing was right. He simply wanted to have a quiet conversation with Vicky and the alarms were annoying him, forcing him to speak louder than necessary. Furthermore, everyone in the OR was accustomed to listening over the alarms and he simply could not afford for them to overhear his conversation with Vicky.

"OH my God!" Little did he know that the patient was wide-awake the whole time and all he truly did by turning off the alarms was to make it easier for Mrs. Robinson to hear them so much more clearer. He surmised it was an exaggerated response to an adequate dose of anesthesia, which would have accounted for the increase in the heart rate and blood pressure he saw. But, it was actually the opposite; it was a full response to little or no anesthesia on board except for a paralytic agent that would have prevented her from moving or speaking at all. It is a response that is usually associated with fear, excruciating pain, and shear terror. The idea of being awake, feeling every stimulation from a simple touch to that cold metallic laryngoscope used to enter the mouth after prying open the mandible upward and forward with one's fingers in order to expose the posterior pharynx below and the Epiglottis must have been a terrifying ordeal.

He thought, "I can assure you that this is neither a gentle nor a painless process and she felt it all. How awful!"

In addition, her mind was wide-awake, directing her body to protest and nothing happened. It got worse; surely someone would recognize that she was not anesthetized and would intervene before feeling the sharp surgical grade steel blade cut her open from stem to stern in a single forceful and deliberate stroke. With time, she was less assured that she would be rescued as she was unable to move a single muscle beyond the minimal occasional eye twitch; it was a sensation well documented in the Medical Literature but few on earth have ever truly experienced it. By the way, she couldn't breathe and was solely dependent on the machine to generously inflate her lungs then deflate them at a set interval, which might or might not have been sufficient for her body's requirement. She could not cry out for help both because she was paralyzed and also because she had this tube deep down her throat, lodged into her trachea irritating the hell out of her windpipe. She wanted to cough it out but she couldn't. All she could do was keep her big girl panties on and simply lie there and take it all! Her brain, heart and lungs were frantically telling her to move, inhale, and stay alive, but her body just laid there, limp as a lump of coal, oblivious to the passage of time and life.

A dichotomy existed between your internal and external persona. Your very existence depended on inhaling oxygen, followed by the exhalation of Carbon Dioxide, a toxin, from the body, no more, no less. But, when paralyzed, you could not move nor will yourself to stay alive beyond three minutes; it was no time at all by all standards but an eternity as you struggled to stay in the present. Deep inside, there was no fear greater than imminent and expected death.

Under normal sequences of a terminal illness, in the face of the grim reaper, apathy would set in well before the brain goes off-line; you just wouldn't care. It was often described as seeing the light, the tunnel, angels from above, being in a euphoric state, awaiting a multitude of virgins and so on. If you were lucky enough—yes lucky—to see someone die, to experience the moment they cross into the afterlife, you would realize and feel the peace that they were enjoying. If you looked carefully, you might have even seen a fleeting smile, a smirk on their face. They no longer feared death, but they readily embraced the end. They pitied you in the real world—you were stuck here as they traversed into the afterlife; 'no more pain and suffering' was the unifying thought. They looked forward to reuniting with their loved ones who had crossed over minutes, days, decades or eons ahead of them—all with a story to tell. The afterlife was a beautiful wonderland that drew them. They gleefully acquiesced. Once you'd experience that, you would no longer fear death.

In this instance however, paralyzed and awake, there was no apathy. It was replaced by sheer unadulterated panic. Every fiber of her existence resisted dying in this unnatural stance. She saw it coming, not a light in the tunnel but a loud locomotive barreling toward her, knowing full well that she could not get out of the way in time. She was trying as hard as humanly possible, but her body pathetically refused to respond, as if challenging her diagnosis of imminent death. Nothing made sense. That sensation was once described to Bill as the feeling of suddenly, and for the first time ever and without any warning, being thrown in the middle of a shark infested ocean with no visible land mass in sight, the water churning every which way and not knowing how to swim.

Her mind registered full well that she was fucked; her remaining innards were all at full attention anticipating that life would cease in the very, very near future, but never fast enough.

Suddenly, every cell in her body realized how precious and precarious life was and they screamed in unison for a reprieve, but no one heard them. The fear of death was the polar opposite to the most primal, eyeball-popping, toe curling orgasm imaginable. As pleasurable as a slowly anticipated climax could be, a premature and imminent death could produce a sensation 180 degrees opposite of that—satiety versus terminal famine.

The dichotomy, on the outside to the untrained eye, looked like no calmer peace. The body simply laid there, in pure blissfulness, the envy of all.

On the inside, her sympathetic nervous system sprang to life. Her heart rate, blood pressure and sweat glands immediately careened out of control. Normally, each heart pulsation would be followed by a wave of oxygenated blood that coursed its way out of the heart and into the great vessels and into smaller and smaller arteries until they terminated into the capillaries then lastly onto each and every cell of your body. They were grateful for the nutrients and in turn, the oxygen triggered a sign to the rest of the body that 'All was well.' In this situation however, these same cells, the greatest processing supercomputer known to mankind, calculated that each wave was bringing less and less oxygenated blood than the previous one while clearing less and less carbon dioxide. They concluded that there would be no real relief coming. This was coupled by the accumulation of every toxin imaginable and, the cells one by one, activated the panic mode. Lactic Acidosis, the worst offender of them all, set in and triggered the ultimate alarm, the fight or flight response. The heart beats faster, harder against your sternum, frantically trying to meet its quota. The cells began to starve and die off, one by one. The vicious cycle continued. She begged for relief, but her request fell on deaf ears. The pain was of such magnitude that she prayed to die immediately; again her behest fell unanswered. She felt every heave of her heart against her ribcage as it struggled; in what her brain now realized was a losing battle. She hoped, no, she pleaded and begged that each heartbeat would mercifully be the last, but they kept on coming.

Her chest hurt more and more with each subsequent heartbeat. Her eyes, the window to her soul, ironically flickered about, focusing on nothing in particular as the image slowly faded to black. Suddenly, she realized that her seemingly pathetic and piss-poor excuse of a life started to flash by in front of her, slowly at first then faster than her vanishing thoughts could accommodate. Her lungs screamed and ached, which was an understatement, as they hungered for the taste of a single molecule of oxygen. Just one last fucking molecule, the only commodity of life it knew.

She would gladly settle for a smog filled breath from the San Fernando Valley on a hot, humid, and hazy day in the month of July; anything was better than nothing.

"Shit," uttered Bill, as he broke away from his painful thoughts. "I treated all of these symptoms with the drug Labetalol which normalized her vital signs. I took away all the clues that could have signaled that something was wrong."

"You fucking schmuck!!"

"I thought all was well when in reality, Mrs. Robinson heard, felt, and experienced it all."

"Again," he thought. "She heard me imply that I would take care of my wife. I'm fucked!"

"The pain she must have felt."

"Fuck her! She's here, ready to implicate me in something that I did not do. Fuck her!" he quietly repeated.

Detective White took it all in.

If that wasn't enough, he thought, as he drifted back to that infamous night, once immobilized, I inflicted more pain as I took my time, shoving that endotracheal tube in her throat, down into her windpipe. As he retraced each and every step, Bill felt the pain of that tube grinding down her windpipe—a sensation he never gave a second thought to until now.

With the tube in place, he remembered taking his time to squeeze that bag and ventilate her. Air, Alas! Oxygenated air was quite a valuable treat. Every cell in her body must have risen and cheered in unison, "WE'RE SAVED!"

The sense of terror abated as her vital signs returned to normalcy with the combination of the drugs Bill had injected and by the clearing of the Carbon Dioxide and other toxins from her body.

Fear was soon replaced by a sense of joy and relief but only for a shortlived moment. Her brain was so grateful for the oxygen that it was receiving that it almost forgot that the rest of the body did not heed any command to move or flee the scene, not even by a millimeter.

Panic, albeit to a lesser degree, returned. She sensed something was still wrong but she felt better with the return of an adequate oxygen level, enough on which for her to survive.

The body was such an oxygen whore that it soon forgot its recent dilemma.

Then she heard the words, "Ready on top Bill?"

Her fear soon escalated as she noticed Bill nodding affirmatively. She heard someone speak the words, "Time Out" and recited her name, medical record number, her condition, allergies, and the procedure they were about to perform. What the hell was that all about?

"Agreed!" Was the response from all in attendance.

Before she could come up with a plausible answer, she heard those two dreaded words she would not soon forget, 'Knife please.'

Before she could fully comprehend what was to come, she felt the full breadth of a number 15 surgical blade cut a path on her abdomen, from her xyphoid process, continuing around her belly button, down to her pubic mound; a standard stem to stern abdominal incision, a prelude to exposing her entire abdominal content.

She screamed!

She thought she did. She must have, of course she did, but no one heard her since no one reacted.

She screamed again, much louder this time with the same result.

She evoked an equivalent sympathetic response as before but on the monitor and to Bill, it registered as a minor annoyance since he had blunted that response with the drug Labetalol.

Her heart rate, followed by her blood pressure, rose to a lesser level. She watched in horror as he reached for the same set of syringes as before. He must have sensed or noticed the consternation in her eyes and replaced them on the cart. Instead, he reached for a roll of clear plastic tape.

"What on earth for?" She thought, as her focus shifted back and forth from the wrenching pain in her belly to the shenanigans of Dr. Presser. She soon found out, as he calmly un-rolled and cut a piece about two inches long and then cut that piece in half again. He reached down and closed both eyelids. He noticed a copious amount of tears escaping from her ducts, yet he still taped them shut.

"She was trying to talk to me, tell me that she was awake and I missed it. Damn it!!" he shouted as he pounded the wall to his right with his left hand. "Fuck!"

Blood spurted out as he reopened the cut from earlier.

"Sorry," he said as he held his hands up in an apologetic posture.

She remembered the feel of the adhesive sticking to her eyelids as he pressed the pieces of tape that effectively rendered her blind to what was to come.

"I can't move, I can't talk and now, I'm blind as a fucking bat!" She screamed to no one in particular, as she could not make any sound at all.

They said when you lose one sense, the others gradually compensated with time. She could only ascertain that her timetable was not long enough for that to happen. All her proprioceptors sprang to life as she felt one—no—two sets of hands tugging at her abdominal wall, ripping it open.

She then surmised something significant must have occurred as all of the alarms fell silent again. That was when she heard the whole conversation with Vicky and how he had a plan to take care of his wife, Kelly.

Dr. Williams forged on with the operation. He finished the incision through a substantial layer of fat; "how embarrassing," she thought even in the midst of all of this pain.

Dr. Williams continued through a layer of connective tissue and muscles using the hot electrical knife, the cautery.

Mrs. Robinson received an unsolicited crash course in human anatomy and surgical instrumentations. She hated each tool in succession. The cautery cut by electrically burning the tissue it comes in contact with.

The smell of burnt flesh took some getting used to, more so when it was yours.

She wasn't sure how much longer she could endure this assault on her sense.

Dr. Williams's surgical advances finally reached the peritoneum, the lining of the abdominal cavity, and excised it in one continuous motion with the Bovey knife.

Excruciating and unrelentless pain flooded every pain fiber in her body. Technically speaking, the peritoneum had no such pain fibers, but everything connected to it does and she could attest that they didn't like to be touched, moved, or cajoled.

"I thought she was anesthetized, but in reality, all I did was immobilized her. Surgery was performed on her while she lay wide-awake. What else could it be?"

"Fuck!" Bill screamed out loud. "This is as humiliating a night as it could ever be."

Fortunately for her, somewhere along the line, he turned on the anesthetic gases and she must have lapsed into a deep anesthetic state. Unfortunately for him, not before she heard his entire soliloquy on how he would 'take care of Kelly.' No amount of drugs or a combination thereof can erase that memory. "You want to tell me the truth now Dr. Presser?" asked Detective White. "This would save us a lot of time, spare a lot of people the discovery process and allow this city, this hospital to move on."

Bill felt each word throb against his temple as he realized that this cunt really thought he was guilty.

"Shit! No! I have nothing more to say other than you are wasting your fucking time with me while the real killer lurks out there!" Suddenly, Bill froze in place.

"Kelly! She's all alone—he can get to her. I must be there for her this time." Bill shot to his feet screaming, "I must get back to the hospital and protect Kelly! Is anyone watching her?"

"RELAX!" was the shout from Detective White, as the two bookend uniforms tackled Bill back down to the chair.

"What a pathetic loser," thought Detective White. He almost sounded believable.

Now that Bill could comprehend the severity of his case, he decided to finally heed the advice of his attorney and clamp down.

"I thought so," was the smart quip from Detective White. "You're a pathetic looser Doc! Nothing short of the chair will do you justice. I will see to that," she said through still clenched teeth.

"Get him the hell out of here!" she exclaimed to the uniforms as she calmly strolled away, tending to her partner.

She reached up and massaged her neck, seemingly still reeling from the imprint of his hands around her throat as she contemplated revenge.

They hauled him away to a different holding cell in a less than pleasant manner. He protested loudly to no one as the treatment intensified all the way down the hall until he was out of ears' shot.

Greg continued the conversation with the detectives and did his best to shift the blame to the boorish interrogating tactics of Detective White. Nonetheless, his vantage point was lost; Bill was not going anywhere.

Meanwhile in the holding cell down the hall, Bill regained his composure and finally took notice of his cellmate.

"What the fuck are you staring at?" he quipped.

Chris, about five inches shorter and fifty pound lighter than Bill, shrank back to the room and simply asked him if he was alright.

They sat silently in their respective corners for what seemed like an eternity until Chris offered him a towel to wrap his once again bleeding hand. Bill reluctantly accepted it and nursed his wound as best as he could. Chris tried to help but a glare from Bill stopped him dead in his tracks.

They finally settled down as if they both were contemplating their respective predicaments.

In the meantime, Greg did his best to mitigate the situation but there was no feigning simplicity. Bill was charged with a multitude of offenses and was scheduled to see the judge in the morning.

Exhausted, sleep overcame Bill in no time.

# Chapter 12

In the morning, Bill was jolted out of his cot and he tried to unruffle himself as best as he could and eventually gave up. He envisioned the constellation of cameras in the courtroom that would record his vagabond demeanor; a long way from his usual and customary life, he thought, frolicking in his well-tailored suits and one of a kind ensembles.

He was shackled and whisked away to face justice. He bid adieu to his cellmate with a nod and was led away, surrounded by four heavily armed guards. Many things ran through his head but nothing still made sense. He desperately wanted an update on Kelly; he knew full well that the critical time for survival was usually the first forty-eight hours after such a brutal attack. He calculated that they were somewhere north of 36 hours and for all he knew; she could be dead by now. He quickly shook that thought, as he knew Kelly to be a fighter, but he himself felt helpless, as he could not protect her in any way shape or form. He was failing her at the basics of his promise to protect her against all outside forces. He grieved silently and grew smaller and more insignificant in stature by the minute.

He was hauled into the courtroom and encountered Greg who had enough time to go home and change into a presentable outfit, ready for the worst. No way his client was ever going to see the light of day, given the events of the last few days; he'd lost count of how many infractions Bill had committed.

They greeted each other and Greg whispered to him what he already knew. He was charged with resisting arrest, assaulting an officer, along with the attempted murder of Kelly and they were still not sure on how he fits in with the murder of Vicky. None of the above would garner him any sympathy from the judge; he would throw the book at him.

Perplexed Bill, muttered, "Vicky? She's dead?" He asked louder than necessary.

The bailiff shot him a look and Bill understood that he was losing points rapidly, again. He froze in place as the gravity of his situation befell on him. That was more than he could handle.

Bill slumped in his chair and sobbed openly, wondering what had become of his orderly and quaint life. Everything was spinning out of control, again.

The uniforms who were gathered around him, anticipating the worst, stiffened as the judge entered the room.

"All rise!" pronounced the Bailiff.

Bill mustered all his energy. The room swayed as he strained to focus on the black robe entering the room from his left to his right.

By training, Bill assumed that all eyes were on him and he quickly regained his composure and stood erect to face the music.

"Good to see you again Dr. Presser, albeit under much different circumstances," boomed a recognizable voice from the bench.

Bill opened his eyes and saw none other than Judge Spiller from his prior court proceedings.

He paused and replied with a feeble voice, "I wish I could say the same your honor," as he tried a fake, yet feeble smile.

In no time, Bill was back in control. Feeling his mojo, his entire body language changed.

His faculty returned and he tried to speak some more but Greg discouraged it with a tug on his upper arm and Bill acquiesced.

The prosecutor, with dearth precision, laid out the charges in front of him. Greg, sensing a losing battle objected at every turn with the weakness of the state charges and requested a continuation or at worst bail for the good doctor, a pillar in the community who was not only innocent but certainly not a flight risk. Judge Spiller was not impressed with the former, recalling their last meeting.

Greg pressed on that the events of record were circumstantial at best. The state had no evidence to support their charges and the occurrences in the precinct were an unfortunate circumstance, a result of the despicable corner the police placed his client. He, in fact planned on filing an unethical claim of rush to judgment against the police department and the detectives of record.

"Save it for the real trial counselor," was the stern reply form the bench. Feeling on a roll, however, Greg continued to poke holes into the prosecution's case and tried in vain to paint his client as the true victim; there was no physical evidence tying his client to the crime. In fact, his client has iron clad alibis covering the purported time line. The prosecution team objected and reminded the defense team that their star witness, Vicky, was dead and was part of the charges against Dr. Presser; and there's the matter of his blood preliminary matching samples collected at bot crime scenes. 'Preliminary' was the operative word and Greg ignored them and carried on. Bill stood there, stoic all the while tuning out the proceeding, still wondering about Kelly.

To everyone's surprise, bail was set at a million dollars and Judge Spiller admonished Bill not to prove him wrong.

The prosecutor vehemently argued to the contrary but Judge Spiller held firm and banged his gavel, indicating the finality of his decision.

An eerie silence befell the court as all, including Greg, wondered what the hell just happened. Bill smiled, at least as best as he could through his disfigured face. Greg leaned over and instructed him as to the expected sequence of events to come and promised him that he should be released by day's end.

"You think you can manage not to screw this up in the meantime?"

Bill nodded in an affirmative way and was taken to his holding cell in preparation for his release.

Unbeknownst to the rest in attendance, Bill's relationship with Judge Spiller goes well beyond their encounter of yesteryears. In fact, Bill was prepared for the judge to recuse himself given their personal connection. However, Bill surmised that the good judge was not ready to reveal that over the years he had supplied Judge Spiller with many illegal prescriptions of Viagra, narcotics, and sedatives to support his voracious sexual appetite.

"How long will it take to discover all of that?" he wondered. "Not my problem for now, I just want to see the sun and smell the proverbial roses," he thought and smiled.

Three hours later, having secured the prerequisite papers and funds, Bill was strolling outside the jail, staring at the sun as if seeing it for the first time. He clutched his belongings contained in a large plastic bag as if they were more valuable than gold. Greg pulled up next to him, in a pristinely detailed black Town Car, rolled down the window and offered him a ride to anywhere.

Not having a specific destination in mind, Bill declined and continued to walk. He turned the corner and immediately realized that this was a part of town in which he was unfamiliar. He turned to look for Greg and take him up on his offer and didn't find him. Greg was already well down the road.

Dejected, Bill forged on.

"Hey," a voice called out to him and he ignored it. "Don't act like you don't remember me Bill, after all, we just spent the night together."

Irritated he turned in anger and saw Chris grinning at him, clutching a similarly matching white plastic bag.

Bill's demeanor softened and they chatted awhile.

"Your first night in the pen?" asked Chris.

Ever the private and calculating man, Bill hesitated, "Somewhat," was his retort. "My life's unraveling and I don't know how the fuck I got here."

"Come on! Come with me. There's a dive around the corner if you're hungry. Let's go eat cause I'm starving; you're buying since you're in a generous spending mood," he said as he pointed his finger at Bill.

That being the best offer he's had in a while, Bill acquiesced and followed Chris.

They walked a few blocks, mostly in silence in a northerly direction. This area was still new to Bill so he took the time to familiarize himself with the route in case he needed to make a quick get away. They ended up in a seedy truck stop diner and they took a booth in the back, by the kitchen. They almost fought for the seat facing the door but Bill, feeling like a guest, ended up with his back to the action. Chris smiled and for once felt superior and in charge.

Surprisingly, at least to Bill, they chatted openly about their respective lives, even though they truly had nothing in common.

Bill found out that Chris was exactly the person he loathed in life, essentially a low life with no aspirations beyond screwing the world because it 'owed him,' an award of fucking society he calls them.

Bill grew angry with Chris and the exchange became contentious at time. The waitress frequently checked in on them even though they were slow to order. It was more an act of self-preservation as she sensed that the conversation could turn ugly on a dime.

Bill managed to cajole out of Chris that he was in for shoplifting and for using a stolen credit card, his Modis Aperandi.

"Wait a minute!" said Chris. "Shouldn't you already know all of this information since you're the one who fucking bailed me out?"

"Why the fuck would I do that?" shouted Bill, regretting the moment he even took this low life up on an invitation for breakfast. Bill was irritated. He fished in his bag, found his wallet and threw down a fifty and proceeded to exit the diner.

Chris jumped up from his seat, knocking over the assorted condiment plate on the table and pleaded with Bill to sit back down. The whole room froze and paid attention to the loud scene in the back of the diner; a brawl was a usual and customary occurrence in this part of town. Things returned to normal as Bill reluctantly sat back down. The crowd resumed their apparent activities and paid little attention to them.

Having regained some sense of control, Chris fished in his jacket and procured what looked like an official court document that indeed listed Bill as the person fronting the requisite assets for a $25K bond on Chris' behalf.

"Weird! There must be a mistake," Bill thought. "Add that to the number of other crazy shit that don't add up today and that would summarize my new life. FML!" He thought as he loudly exhaled.

When things settled down, Bill, in turn gave Chris the short version of the events leading to their encounter in the holding cell. He grew insensibly upset as he recounted his dilemma and professed his innocence; Chris, being a lifer, was not swayed, everyone was innocent in the big house, his smirk divulged.

Having had enough of Chris, Bill gathered his stuff, this time being aware of his consummate public persona, took notice of his surroundings and searched for a quieter exit. They exchanged contact info and graciously departed but not before a few patrons recognized him as the newsmaker that he had become.

It took Bill a while to make his way to the impound lot, which was located closer to the courthouse he left earlier. They would not release his car. Ugh! He now felt the full weight of the alleged conspiracy transpiring over him and walked out without so much of a response.

Still fuming, Bill recalled the words of his attorney and maintained his demeanor. He departed and located a rental car agency down the street and secured a Ford Taurus. "How common has my life become in such a short while," he mused.

With nowhere to go, Bill pulled out of the rental car lot and meandered about downtown until he found himself on the 41 freeway, heading home. To his surprise, it didn't take him long before he turned the corner to the house. What he saw, he was not expecting. There were at least 10 people, all in official garbs milling about his front and back yards, in search of something. Nonetheless, they seemed determined to find whatever it was that they were looking for. Several marked and unmarked cars and vans were haphazardly parked in his driveway and lawn; he was not happy.

"I pay good fucking money to keep that grass green," he yelled to no one in particular, as he slammed an open palm on the steering wheel. Fortunately, the horn did not go off.

There was yellow tape strewn about all entry points and he made an executive decision to bypass the house as it was unlikely that they would let him in. He recalled the scene at Vicky's place and opted for a U-turn and departed in the opposite direction.

Feeling much the man without a country, Bill wandered about town until he settled on a course for the hospital. The sun was slowly settling over the horizon to its nightly position and the gloomy sky reflected his mood. There was enough of a breeze for him to miss his favorite jacket in the back of his car, still at the fucking impound lot.

Bill felt numb. He was in a trance that forbade him to address his difficulties. He was soon on auto pilot and didn't quite recall how he made it all the way to the hospital. Not feeling his usual and customary chipper self, he opted for a common parking space, bypassing his own spot with the plaque he loved to admire and pat everyday. Not today, he thought, not today, as he sidestepped the usual entryway.

He was not quite sure how to proceed from here. He desperately needed to see Kelly but he was unsure of the scene that would await him in the ICU. He took the back stairs, hoping to escape all human contact and made his way to the Operating Room. He arrived via the back entry point and hesitated when he heard the commotion emanating from within. He tiptoed to the door, and slowly pushed it open enough to see the collection of suits inside. He didn't recognize anyone but Detective White who had her back to him and was engaged in a poignant conversation with Sheila.

Bill strained to hear their words but could not make them out. He thought about bursting in and joining the party, surprising all, but his confidence, waning to all time low, a place he barely recalled since his bashful days as a teen, paralyzed him in place.

He must not have been as still as he thought because Sheila, facing him while still chatting with Detective White who in turn, was busy writing in her note pad and therefore missed Sheila's surprised look when she snapped her head toward Bill. Her eyes steeled and her body tensed.

Several in attendance read her body language and followed her eyes toward the door. Fortunately, their viewing angle precluded them from seeing who or what captivated Sheila so much.

Detective White, ever aware of her surroundings, sensed the disturbance and in one motion, stopped writing, looked up at Sheila and equally trailed her eyes to the door. Her viewing angle however, better than her timing was a hair too slow as she barely missed catching full sight of Bill, as he retreated behind the closing doors.

Her gaze returned to Sheila who tried to recover but her nervousness betrayed her. Unbeknownst to Bill, Detective White and her entourage were there to question and possibly apprehend him once again; apparently new evidence contrary to his innocence had surfaced. The final blood analysis from Vicky's crime scene matched with the blood recovered from Kelly's crime scene and unfortunately, to him.

Detective White motioned ever so slightly with a nod of her head and the two suits accompanying her moved toward the back door. With hands resting on their service revolvers, they slowly approached the door and had their guns fully extended by the time they made their way into the stairwell. It was empty. They slowly approached the railing, looked up and down, and saw nothing afoul so they returned and reported to Detective White. Bill vanished in time. He waited for the coast to clear before moving on. The conversation between Sheila and Detective White resumed and shortly thereafter, the convoy departed and Sheila made her way back to her office. To her surprise, she found the door ajar.

"I never leave my door open and in fact, I remembered locking it before stepping out to the front desk to talk to the detectives," she thought to herself. She paused at the entryway, trying to ascertain whose leg is that in her office.

"For crying out loud, come in before I'm seen," boomed Bill from within.

"How the hell did you get in?" quipped Sheila as her voice trailed off, remembering that Bill was legendary at getting into places that he should never have had access to. In fact, that's really how they first met. The young Dr. Presser was caught in the sub sterile room in the OR, an area he should not have access to, banging a new hire who also had no business being in that location. Sheila stumbled in on his entire seduction of this new tech and must have admitted, she too was duly impressed with Bill's approach and she too would have fallen for the young Dr. Presser in her youth.

She sat back and watched the whole thing unfold. She got to witness Bill's sexual prowess first hand, again. She enjoyed the scenery and she waited until the last possible moment to walk closer to them just as they both fell over, gasping and climaxing. She simply stood over them, waited for them to open their eyes. The young tech regained her composure much quicker than Bill and hastily tried to scamper out of the room. She managed to straighten out her scrub top and pull up her panties and scrub bottoms all the while fishing for her lab coat that hung on the hook behind the door before she quickly departed. Bill on the other hand simply grinned, as Sheila couldn't take her eyes off of his still oozing member.

Shaken back to reality, Sheila quickly entered the room and closed the door. She took stock of his disheveled appearance and immediately felt pity for him. They sat in silence for a while and she eventually asked if he was ok and aware of the heap of trouble that he was in.

No reply.

"Your blood Bill. Your blood was recovered all over the crime scenes; both at your house and at Vicky's murder site Bill. They really believe that you had something to do with all of this mess Bill. Do you?"

He simply glared at her. She believed him.

Sheila recounted to Bill the extent of Kelly's injuries and for the first time, Bill actually comprehended the severity of Kelly's situation. She probably would not survive this, his medical training quickly translated.

"Someone must be truly pissed off at me to the point that they would take it out on Kelly. She would never hurt a fly," he thought. "This is definitely directed at me." The list of enemies he'd cultivated over the years was so long that he did not know where to begin.

"This makes no sense, Sheila!" he proclaimed through gritted teeth.

Bill slumped over, head in hand trying to control his anger and equally important, to shield his misting eyes from Sheila. Bill wanted to visit Kelly in the ICU but was dissuaded by Sheila, given the commotion that his presence would cause. She promised that she would find out all she could and call him later with an update.

He thanked her and scurried out of her office, out the back door, and to the quiet space of his rented Taurus. He sat there behind the wheel in bewilderment and plotted out his next course of action; driving away was all he came up with. Feeling lost, Bill left the parking lot and was soon back on the road, navigating the back streets of the city, trying to remain invisible.

He drove aimlessly and soon was on the proverbial other side of the track, staring at the uneven neon light of the 'G GO C UB' although it took some time and imagination to see that it really spelled out 'GOGO CLUB,' as he got close enough to see the unlit and missing background letters.

Bill circled the block several times before running out of excuses not to attend. Lord knows he could use the distraction. It'd been years since he needed the services offered on the other side of these doors. "I've had more than my fair share from the hospital," he thought. But today, it was more about disappearing rather than just seeking the pleasure of a stranger.

He located the parking lot on the far right side of the building and pulled in. For the first time, he was grateful that he was in this nondescript automobile and haphazardly parked, taking up two spaces. Still the rebel, Bill found it hard to conform, even in these trying times. That was simply his way of maintaining control even though he was now a marked man, Fresno's public enemy number one.

"How the hell did I get here?" Bill slowly dragged himself out of the car, feeling conflicted about even being seen at the topless club while his wife clanged on for dear life; too late for that, he was already spotted. In fact, if he was not too preoccupied with is own pity-party, he would have spotted the black truck that had been following him ever since he left the jail, digitally recording his every move.

Keeping his head down, his face expressionless, Bill paid the requisite fare and entered the club. The music was much louder and the lights were far dimmer than they needed to be. His eyes eventually adjusted and he barely made out the bar on the left; the main stage with its obligatory pole dancer was dead center with a circle of captivating patrons around it and a lesser stage and private seating area to the right. He made out a shadowy figure navigating the small stage completely devoid of an audience and settled on privacy and made his way to the small platform on the right. No sooner than when he sat down and eased in the big comfortable easy chair with the high side arms and back, the necessities for an engaging lap dance, he was approached by the scantily dressed waitress who simply said, "What will it be hon?"

"Water please," was the curt and almost inaudible reply.

"You're gonna have to down a few gallons of water sweets if you plan on getting your money's worth tonight. This area gets a minimum of 3 drinks at 20 bucks a pop or 2 lap dances. Your call Honey," she said through a fake southern drawl.

He was about to reply when the dancer came off the stage and approached them.

"It's OK Tammy Tam, get the man some water. I know him; he's an old customer," she lied. Tammy hesitated but eventually sauntered out of the area. Now alone, the dancer made her way to Bill in a very deliberate and suggestive manner.

Very seldom did she get a solo guest all to herself; unless you count the attentive man at the bar keeping track of their every movement. She couldn't fully see Bill given the lighting and his sitting position but she figured she would always have the upper hand on any man. The dancer figured she could cajole a sizable tip out of him given the remoteness of the area. "No man can resist my seductive powers," she thought.

As she drew closer, she noticed that she had Bill's full attention. He hadn't planned on this.

He simply wanted to hide and clear his head but now this voluptuous silhouette's got his nostrils flaring and his loins a stirring.

"Wow!" He thought, that was a quick response. That was very unlike him to get a hard on in a place like this; it was so impersonal he always thought but this chick got him.

He straightened himself in the chair and leaned forward. After what seemed like an eternity she closed the gap between them, took full stock of Bill and to both their surprise she said, "Well!" She paused for effect. "It's so good to see you Dr. Presser. I didn't know this was your kind of establishment," she said in a distinctive British accent.

Bill's face betrayed him, perplexed as to how this dancer could possibly know him but he must admit that voice, actually, her accent stuck a chord of recognition but from where? She smirked at his recognition.

She leaned over, kissed him on the cheek and purposefully maintained tactile connection with him as she rolled over and sat next to him, never loosing eye contact or her wry smile.

He closed his eyes and held his breath. She was amused. He slowly exhaled, recollecting the last time a woman left him so breathless. She giggled ever so gently. He inhaled her intoxicating aroma and almost succumbed to her powers but much to her dismay, he inexplicably broke her trance and sat up erectly.

His thoughts cleared and he remembered that she had called him by his government name earlier.

Inquisitively, he stared intently at her until the image in front of him transformed into a person with a name, a location, along with many prior interactions. Sheepishly he recognized her and quickly gathered his stuff and started to leave but she reached out, grabbed his arm and politely protested and asked him to please stay.

He softened. He has never been able to resist her proper, well-cultured British accent in the past and he awkwardly retraced his steps back to the easy chair.

Tammy Tam returned with his water and he added a Vodka Martini to the order along with whatever Alex the dancer, his old acquaintance was drinking.

Much to his feeble protest, Bill was soon in the midst of a lap dance with Alex who now informed him that her stage name is Sexxi Lexxi; he was not impressed. It was funny how she'd grown to hate that moniker when her friends call her that and now finally, she'd met someone who agreed with her that it was really a cheesy porn star name.

"I like this side of him," she giggled to no one in particular.

# Chapter 13

Thus began the first Seduction of Lexxi.

Bill was thoroughly distracted despite her MANY futile attempts at seducing him. He recalled the first and many times he'd come to her department, Medical Records, located in the bowels of the hospital. It was a grim and dank repository for everything written within the hospital. It was also the place where all doctors eventually ended up to complete their records, either with a simple signature of a verbal order or to close out their delinquent entries on a procedure or a patient encounter. The absence of any of the above would preclude full reimbursement from the insurance companies, including Medicare. Bill was a frequent visitor. She sometimes fantasized that he deliberately failed to complete his charts, and he had more than any other physicians at the facility just so he could come interact with her in a far and remote area, away from the prying eyes of his other concubines. She knew of his feral reputation, yet he was always pleasant and respectful to her. He would hang on to every word she spoke and one day, he finally admitted that he found her accent quite intoxicating. He later asked her if she had a boyfriend and she immediately replied, "Yes," she lied.

"A lucky man," he replied, smiled, and never inquired again. She found him intriguing, yet she was disappointed that she had so quickly rebuked his apparent advance or was it simply banter? She often wished she had not pushed him away and knew it would end differently if there ever were a next time. She'd overheard many conversations about his boorish behavior and conquests but she always defended him as the quintessential gentleman. Thus began the rumors that she, someday, would be his next acquisition. That day never came until today. She had finally gotten the legendary Bill Presser in front of her and she was not going to miss out on the opportunity to seduce him.

Much to her dismay, Bill was not responding to her relentless advances. He even seemed to drift in and out of consciousness right before her eyes.

"You should go home!" She proclaimed loudly, and pushed away from him. That seemed to snap him to attention.

"I don't have a home to go to," he replied in a deflated tone.

Surprised by his answer, she actually felt sorry for him and simply stared at him. He was a handsome man with chiseled features that she found endearing and attractive.

She should walk away but couldn't.

"Why not? You pissed off the Mrs. Again?"

He fleetingly glared at her then slumped back to the chair and exhaled loudly.

"Is he gonna cry on me?" This hulking man in front of her appeared deflated, vulnerable, and on his last option. He was quite the contrarian from his usual character.

She thought it, dismissed it, looked around, and couldn't believe the words coming out of her mouth.

"Listen," she said, "I don't normally do this. I'm just not that kind of girl, but it's slow here tonight. Buy me out and you can crash at my place; you look like you could use a friend and a good night sleep."

Not recalling the last time he actually had a good night sleep or a friend for that matter, he searched her face for a hint of a scam and he did not find any. She held his gaze, sensing that he was contemplating her offer, stood up, and pulled him to his feet.

"Pay that man in the cheap suit by the door," she said. "I'll go change and meet you by the front door." Still half-witted, he looked in the direction of the door and back at her. She smiled, spun him around and gently ushered him to the man in the oversized suit. They talked awhile and Bill searched his pockets for his billfold. Remembering that he had it out by the stage, he turned to fetch it but Lexxi produced it from her bra and handed it to him. She kissed him on the cheek and whispered that she will be gone for less than five minutes.

"You think you can manage to stay awake for that long big guy?" He nodded affirmatively and she scampered off to the dressing room and soon disappeared around the corner. The suited guy collected the necessary fare and admonished him to behave himself. "She's a special girl," he added.

Lexxi returned a lot faster than the allocated five minutes but then again, time meant nothing to him at this moment.

They departed and Bill lumbered next to her in silence. They got in his car; she was impressed that he held the door open for her.

He drove her to her car in the lot across the street and followed her all the way to her apartment on Bleecker Street. He'd lived in Fresno for the better part of eight years and had never been to any part of town that he had travelled today. Her side of the city was not an exception but he found it quite livable.

They made it to her building and took the elevator to the third floor. They made a right turn at the fork and she handed him her bag and fetched her keys from her purse and unlocked the double locks to her door.

His pursuer in the black truck pulled up just in time to see them as they entered the elevator. He quickly made his way to see it stop on the third floor. He scanned the registry located by the front door and made notation of the only girl's name out of the three units on that floor. He returned to his truck.

Bill held the door open for Lexxi and he followed her in not knowing what to expect. He was duly impressed with the lavish yet purposeful modern decoration; he didn't see that coming.

She ushered him to a seat in the living area and offered him a cocktail, wine actually as she was not accustomed to heavy liquor and didn't see the point of keeping an ample supply. She couldn't recall the last visitor to her apartment since her mom last called on her over a year ago.

By the time she opened a new bottle, selected the appropriate glasses and returned to him, Bill was fast asleep with his head slumped over his chest; she smiled and pitied him at the same time.

She poured herself a glass, drained it and refilled it and set the bottle on the dining table. She made her way to her bedroom, stripped, showered, donned something sexy but not too provocative and returned to find him in the same position she left him.

She tried to gently usher him in a supine position but he woke up, confused as to his whereabouts. Having regained his faculties, he was surprised to see her entirely in a different attire; he frowned.

"How long was I asleep for?"

"Awhile," she replied.

She offered him a glass of wine; he accepted it and he too drained it in one swallow.

They stared at each other and she broke the silence by offering him her bed, as he was much too tall for her sofa. He tried to protest but she grabbed his hands and led him to the bedroom.

He stood there in place, not knowing what to do next. She smiled and slowly began to undress him. He offered no resistance.

She was surprised how muscular and firm his whole body was. In no time, he was down to his boxers and wondered if she would take them off too, unsure if he would draw the line at that; she didn't and he was disappointed. She pulled back the covers and he lay down, crumpled the pillow under his head and was fast asleep by the second breath.

She stood at the door for a while, watching how vulnerable yet comfortable he was; she smiled. She picked his clothes off the floor and took notice of the heaviness of his pants. She searched though the pockets, removing its contents, keys, a gate card-hospital fare, a wallet with a thick wad of bills of nothing but hundreds. She thought about pocketing the wad and thought better of it and placed the bounty on the nightstand next to him. She then went to the closet for the obligatory bedding materials and retreated to the living room. Wide-awake, she consumed the remainder of the wine and soon found herself groggy enough to curl up on the sofa and she crashed hard.

She was jolted from her slumber, many hours later by Bill's thrashing about and moaning in the other room.

She checked the clock in the kitchen, 05:33. She made her way to the door and found him fast asleep again, this time all the covers removed, and he, naked for the world to see. She took stock of his incredible physique but focused on his flaccid yet full penis. She imagined how much larger it could get with the right persuasion. It didn't take long for her to find out as he rolled over and ended up in a fetal position with his hand neatly tucked between his legs. He rolled again, this time exposing his ever-expanding morning erection. She gasped. Unsure what to do next, recalling the old saying, never waste a good hard on. She slowly advanced, not wanting to spook him awake, at least not yet.

She stood at bedside and admired this fully circumcised specimen that can thrill her to her full delight. Having seen and felt so many cocks in her line of duty, she knew this one was special. She could feel the wetness welling up inside her thighs and knew right then and there that she wanted to feel him thrusting deep inside her. She sized him up. He was bigger than she'd ever had and her excitement grew even wilder. She wanted him. She envisioned wrapping her lips around his cock; she momentarily closed her eyes at that thought.

"Impressed?" she heard him say, jarring her out of her fantasy. Before she could reply, he reached out, grabbed her by her arm and yanked her into the bed on top of him; she offered no resistance.

## THE SECOND SEDUCTION OF LEXXI

Thus began the true seduction of Lexxi in ways she never imagined was ever possible. He held her gaze momentarily in what seemed like an eternity to her. He had her arms firmly wrapped around and pinned to the small of her back and he gently coaxed her towards him, she paused then relented and kissed him ever so softly on his lips.

She watched him close his eyes and moan. She smiled; she knew that she had him. Mr. Control Freak was about to have the tables turned on him.

She managed to free her hands and pushed off of him. She moved his arms into that crucifix position. "No touching," she whispered. He complied, barely. He started to move and she stopped him with a light slap on the hands.

"No no no," she playfully said while wagging her index finger near his nose. "Am I gonna have to pull out the handcuffs and restrain you?" He thought about it, acquiesced and allowed his arms to flop over onto the bed again. "Good boy," she whispered.

By now, she was up on her elbows again, planning her assault on his body. She began with light and wet kisses from his chin down his neck and stopped on his right nipple and bit. He shuttered and she giggled.

She bit harder and his body shook to near convulsion. She took her time moving to the left nipple and repeated her movements; this time with more determination and intensity. Bill was beside himself trying not to reach for her. Each time he started to move, she would simply pat his hands back down to their resting position, far away from her. Again, she admonished him with a bite to lie still; no touching allowed. She blew in his direction without looking up.

She continued her trek to where the ultimate prize that anxiously awaited her. Judging by the amount of time she was taking, you would think that it would have been a run of the mill trophy at the end of her journey. "No," she thought. "This is turning into a battle of will. Who will blink first?"

She doubled down, knowing she was fully in charge. He won't last long. She continued; his body still twitched each time she kissed a new spot. His brain tried to anticipate each move but she selfishly kept him guessing and he mistimed the subsequent kiss every time; so, the twitching continued.

The anticipation was killing him. Now it became a game, him reaching out for her and she patting, now slapping is hands away. He figured eventually, she would relent. He imagined where he would touch first. He'd eyed her firm breasts all evening and was planning on trespassing on them the first chance he got.

The energy in the room was simply amazing, she thought. When she made it all the way down to his crotch, she confirmed that her slow and deliberate approach had him at full attention, erection. "Can this thing grow any bigger?" She wondered.

She slowly wrapped her left hand around the base, than she repeated the same action just above that with her right hand.

"Damn!" There was still plenty of exposed dick left to satisfy most women. This is no longer a legendary story, she thought. She squeezed him with both hands, confirming that this indeed was real and she was front and center to what was about to happen next.

She looked up at him and he was oblivious to her thoughts and stare. His deep rhythmic breathing simply conveyed that he was enjoying the moment.

Sensing her glare and inactivity, Bill slowly lifted his head off the pillow and opened his eyes and looked directly into her eyes. Matching his gaze, Lexxi smiled, opened her mouth as wide she could and smoothly and continuously took him in, releasing each hand, one at a time as she made her way all the way down to his scrotum.

Bill was amazed at her skills. He completely disappeared inside her mouth and she didn't even show a hint of discomfort. She must have read his mind as she forged on for good measure.

This was a never felt before sensation that had his brain screaming in ecstasy. "How long can I last, he mused?"

About to loose control, Bill wanted to regain his composure but he felt so good in her mouth. He felt the tension building in his feet and knew it couldn't be long before he lost himself. "I can't let that happen," he thought with a sense of urgency.

Still paralyzed with ecstasy, Bill summoned all his energy and grabbed her by the arms pressed her up above him and in one motion and flipped her onto her abdomen. Now with her body in a full prone position, he first coaxed her upon her knees and then pressed her torso against the backboard with her arms fully extended above her head and pinned to the wall with his left hand. He leaned into her and whispered, "My turn."

He kissed her on the nape of her neck and soon lost himself in her aroma. He caught himself and resumed his task. She tried to release her arms from his grip and he spanked her ass lightly with his free right hand and she jumped.

"There's more where that came from," he coyly informed her. She wiggled in place, indicating she would gladly goad him into punishing her some more.

He reached around and gently cupped her right breast and firmly pinched her nipple. She feigned pain and cowered into him; he was pleased.

He felt his loin throb with each pinch, squeeze. Having waited long enough, he let go of her breast, reached down and in one motion, grabbed and shoved his fully erect penis into her. Given his legendary endowment, Bill was expecting some form of friction on initial penetration but to his amazement, he slid deep into her without much resistance. He was duly impressed on how well lubricated she was. Her juice freely splattered about with each thrust.

At first, she simply whimpered, not wanting to let on that he was hurting her because he felt so damn good inside her.

After a while, she couldn't contain herself and her uncontrollable screams freely flowed and could be heard throughout the building. She briefly envisioned the sly look she would garner from her neighbors in the days to come.

"Fuck em! They probably wish they could be me."

The dance continued to the tune of the rocking headboard, threatening to come apart at any moment but it mercifully held its form until they both unleashed a blood-curdling scream as they simultaneously climaxed, convulsed, and collapsed haphazardly onto the bed. By the end, as they found themselves on the edge of the bed, nearly falling out of it, they both took stock of their predicament and laughed out loud. After that, they laid in complete silence, save for their labored breathing. The smell of sex was all over the room; neither one commented or complained.

Exhausted, they both curled up on the bed, panting out loud until her respiration eventually slowed to almost nothing while soon after, his reached a bronchial crescendo that eventually woke her up. She smiled at that thought and eased her way out of bed with minimal interruption of his respiratory effort. She made her way to the kitchen, turned on the coffee maker at first, the TV next, and fetched a glass of room temperature water, trying to replenish the copious amount of sweat she just expanded.

She was in a good place. She replayed the events of the last 12 hours and although way past her comfort zone, she was glad that she took a leap of faith and engaged the good Dr. Presser. Many things crossed her mind, primarily his wife, their joint work place but worst of all, her little dirty secretive life style at the GOGO CLUB. How would that fit in?

"We'll cross that part at a later time," she thought. "For now, he's mine to lose and I intend on hanging on. This side of me he knows does not represent who I really am. Funny how many times I've said that I'm ready to leave this lifestyle but never had a good reason to do so. The money was good and I've never cared about any one enough to do that nuclear family shit. Now THAT is not I," she lied.

"Look at you," she thought. "One good fuck session and you're enthralled, conjuring up a life that is unattainable. He's a married man and, not sure which is worse, that or a man whore?"

She sighed and filled her coffee mug with the dark elixir and a hint of cream and continued to the sofa in front of the TV. She flicked channels until she realized that she went by a facsimile of Bill, 2 channels ago. She clicked back and froze at the image, lead story of the morning again recounting the exploits of and the just issued arrest warrant for one William A. Presser, M.D. for the initial attempted murder of his wife and now, also the murder of his mistress. The reporter meticulously laid out the case against him and Lexxi had to admit, it was quite damning. The news anchor reported that the blood recovered from both crime scenes were a perfect match for Bill. Lexxi wept silently. She felt so stupid for having trusted him.

His behavior at the club last night now made even more sense. How could he so passionately take her like he did this morning with the weight of all this gruesomeness on his mind? What kind of monster is this man?

She remained in place, not knowing what to do, where to go.

Truth be told, there was only one thing to do and with a heavy heart, she reached for the phone. She dialed the number on the screen. After 2 rings, a woman with a deep gravel voice answered it; an obvious smoker, she thought. She sounded much like Lexxi's grandmother before she past away from COPD.

She informed the operator that she had information germane to the murder being featured on TV. She further allowed herself to reveal that Dr. Presser was with her, in her home.

The operator asked her to hold, partly to trace her number, partly to get Detective White on the Phone. While she waited, it dawned on her that she was so consumed with the task at hand that she no longer heard Bill's snoring from the bedroom. A sense of panic overcame her and she turned to go check up on him and almost bumped into him. Sheer dread overcame her as she fell backwards over the chair and onto the floor. Detective White overheard the commotion and peppered her with a deluge of questions as she was putting on her holster with her 9 mm Glock, fully loaded. In one motion, she reached for her jacket and continued out of the door.

"Is all ok? Are you safe? Is he still there with you? Is he harming you?"

"Yes! No," she stammered, "I'm ok."

"Don't hang up; play it cool," Detective White told her, "Say, 'It's all good' with a smile if he's near you."

With hesitation, Lexxi repeated the phrase but couldn't muster a smile. She stared at him in shear terror, regretting that she even made the phone call.

Befuddled, Bill searched her face for an answer.

To his surprise, she said loud enough to be heard over the telephone, that she was on the phone with the police and that they were on their way to arrest him for trying to murder his wife. He should leave and not hurt her. "I'm sorry," she added with sincerity.

Confused, he turned to the TV and heard the recap. The weight of the news was all that he could handle. Bill wept openly, professing his innocence to Lexxi. She stared at him and her eyes continued to his hand, still sporting that blood stained gauze he had from before.

"Why had I not noticed that before?" she admonished herself. He trailed her eyes to his hand and held it up, trying to explain.

"It's not what you think!" he screamed. "I cut my hand on a glass at home. You have to believe me! I love her," he managed to get out through a snotty-bubbly-nose sob.

"Why would I kill her? Oh my god!" He shouted as the words resonated in his head.

Lexxi, equally confused, dropped the phone as she heard Detective White's fading voice, begging her to stay on the phone with her.

She got up and slowly walked over to Bill who by now was bent over the sink, puking his guts out. She placed a hand on his shoulder and lightly made slow and small deliberate circles with her palm.

"I'm sorry," she said. "I'm sorry but they made you sound so guilty Doc," she apologetically said in a low monotonous voice. "Maybe you should leave. The police will be here anytime soon; go!" she exclaimed, "please."

Bill contemplated his options, got dressed, thanked her profusely, and promised to clear his name.

"I'll come back for you," he added with a wry smile. They hugged and he departed.

He could hear the sirens as he got to the sidewalk. He quickly made it to his rental, opened the door and slid in by the time the two wailing cruisers whizzed by him and stopped four doors down from his nondescript Taurus.

Bill caught a glimpse of a black truck that peeled away as the squad cars pulled up. In fact, one of the cruisers chased it down and disappeared around the corner.

Weird.

"Thank you," he said to no one.

They probably assumed that it was Bill in that truck trying to make a clean getaway. He was about to start the car when he spotted a Crown Vic cruising towards him. He again slumped down just in time to see Detectives White and Afoot, the latter still in a sling, scamper by him to join the others.

Good thing he was in this POS of a car and that they were in such a rush, otherwise he would have been toast.

Bill waited for the cavalry to enter the building before he started the car and pulled away to his favorite destination, nowhere.

# Chapter 14

By the time the police had arrived at her unit, Lexxi was dressed in a simple silky Japanese style robe and waited for them by the front door of her apartment. Detective White was surging ahead of the uniforms when she spotted Lexxi's body language and assumed they missed Bill; she couldn't contain her disappointment as she slowed down to a deliberate pace.

"Is he gone?" she queried.

Lexxi simply and affirmatively shook her head.

"Come in," she said as she pivoted into her apartment.

Now in her apartment, Detective White quizzed her as to the events of last night. Lexxi gleefully recounted the events of the night, save for the sex. That was none of their fucking business her betraying smile told them.

Not pleased by her obvious omissions as the room still reeked of a steaming sexual session, Detective White pummeled Lexxi with more poignant questions. Lexxi stuck to her narrative.

Detective White's stare was interrupted by a buzzing sound; she patted herself and retrieved her phone and connected the call.

The caller on the other end relayed to her that Mrs. Robinson was found in her room dead, gutted in similar fashion, as was Kelly. They described the area as a gruesome, bloody and a violent murder scene and the regress of the perpetrator was caught on the grainy surveillance cameras. The perp eerily matches the description of the orderly seen milling about her room earlier that day. The time of her demise was placed somewhere around 2am, a time that would seemingly exonerate Bill as the attacker if Lexxi's account of the night were to be believed.

"Shit!" she exclaimed as she disconnected the call.

Her attention turned back to Lexxi and the interrogation continued for the better part of the next hour and her story never wavered.

The neighbors, all of those who were available, were equally questioned and they corroborated Lexxi's story and then some. They added the loud feral noises they heard earlier that morning, preceded by Bill and Lexxi's arrival at about midnight.

"Something's not adding up," thought Detective White. "How could anyone else know about Mrs. Robinson's recall and her importance to this case? What's the connection?"

She quickly left the apartment with the usual admonishment to Lexxi to update her as to any other information pertaining to last night's events, especially if she hears from the good Dr. Presser.

Detective White made her way back to the hospital and took notice of Mrs. Robinson's murder room. How was it possible that no one took stock of the noise, the mayhem that ensued? The CSI team meticulously processed the scene and she personally interviewed as many of the staff as she could. It didn't take her long to figure out that the story of Mrs. Robinson's travails during her surgery were gossip #1 at the hospital. Everyone knew of her recall and the trauma she experienced the night before. Most hospitals prided themselves in secrecy and patients' privacy, but this one was quite abuzz with such a rare and unfortunate event. All within, violated the basic tenets of HIPPA laws, which dictate to say nothing to anyone not directly involved in the case, even family members.

It was clear to Detective White that it was absolutely possible that everyone, even Dr. Presser, was fully aware of the events and ordeals that befell the unfortunate Mrs. Robinson.

"Shit! Back to square one," she thought. "Again, if that stripper is to be believed then the timeline doesn't make any sense. Right now, nothing contradicts her." She was forced to now contemplate a different person of interest or find an accomplice. This was going from open and shut to convoluted. Shit!

With the proper samples collected and all possible personnel interviewed, Detective White departed and headed home after reviewing the security tapes that only confirmed that she indeed did come in close contact with the assailant. She cursed at herself for not picking up on it. However, it'd been an exhausting few days. It was time for some much needed rest.

"Let's regroup later on," she said knowing full well that the body count was just beginning and she didn't have a handle on anything; she hated that feeling.

She made it home, mentally drained. She showered, fixed a Gin and Tonic, curled up in her easy chair and tried to review the case file while her neglected cat, Simon, milled about her feet. She was soon asleep and her fastidious slumber was eventually interrupted.

"1 pm, Wow!" she exclaimed, as she checked the home screen on her ringing cell phone. It was the lab; she recognized the number; apparently they had been trying to get a hold of her for some time now but she'd been sound asleep.

She listened attentively and was informed that the preliminary report from the hospital drew a hit from the data bank. The blood collected from the bed and the body plus a single fingerprint recovered from the IV bag matched an assailant known as Christopher Mathews. He was a low level petty criminal who was well known to law enforcement with an extensive rap sheet but this crime is well out of his usual M.O.

Several things caught her attention.

What was his obvious connection to all of this and why a single fingerprint? The latter bothered her.

She searched her memory bank and distinctly remembers the orderly wearing gloves. Weird!

She gathered herself, refilled Simon's food bowl, drained the rest of her drink, and left for the office.

Once there, she pulled up the file on Christopher and familiarized herself with his extensive record.

She got to the end and made an unexpected discovery. Apparently Christopher, arrested for shoplifting, was in the same holding cell with the good doctor the night prior. Her heart raced as she connected the dots.

"Got ya!" she exclaimed exuberantly. "What a dumb and obvious move," she thought. Bill didn't need to be at the hospital to kill Mrs. Robinson, an obvious thorn on his side. He had the perfect accomplice to do his bidding.

How stupid was he to leave such glaring evidence behind? "Amateur," she thought. This job would be so much harder if she only dealt with professionals. Truth be told, idiots with no forethought or adequate planning committed most crimes.

"Don't they watch TV to know that we're always watching and are two steps ahead of them? Thank you morons!" she blew out.

She continued to thumb through the file and located the receipt for Chris' bail money put up by the one and only Dr. Presser.

"How fucking stupid," her one-track mind recorded. "Finally, this picture is clearing up. The bastard has been feigning his innocence all the while as he methodically tried to cover his track. I look forward to nailing him! This will be her crowning jewel of a case, tailor made for the death penalty. This cold-blooded doctor will pay for his murderous endeavors. What the fuck happened to just divorcing your wife? No, that wasn't good enough; he had to permanently dispose of her. What a fucking monster!" she exclaimed as she closed and slapped Chris' file on the table and gathered her coat and glock, and made her way through the precinct. She found her partner, filled him in on the details, collected the obligatory info on Chris' last known address, and amassed a small yet competent back up team.

Deep down however, she knew that this was all too tidy but she forged on anyway.

"Let's bring him in," she said. "I want him alive at all costs. Remember, it's the good doctor that we want! After we pick Chris up, he'll sing like a canary."

The ride to Chris' place was surreally quiet as they made their way to the south side of town. Arriving at the small and desolate apartment building, they formulated a plan and stormed the entrance in a methodical way.

They weren't expecting what they found.

Chris was sitting in a wretched side chair, mouth agape with a single and well-defined bullet hole in the middle of his forehead. Blood was clearly oozing from him, signaling a recent injury, a sign not lost on the team as they quickly fanned across the rooms in search of the assailant. Nothing.

The team made their way out of the apartment, just in time to catch the back of a dark colored truck leaving the scene, much faster than the rest of the traffic.

"Fuck! A hair late again," Detective White shouted to no one in particular.

Deflated, she disbanded the team and made her way back to her cruiser and sent out a non-descriptive APB on the truck, knowing full well that it was purely an exercise in futility.

# Chapter 15

Bill, having recently awakened from his slumber in the shopping mall parking lot, was now 30 minutes into his aimless drive about town. He settled in on a bar/diner on Herndon, contemplating his next move. He thought about calling Lexxi but surmised that she was under surveillance and abandoned that idea. Feeling all-alone, he settled for some much needed food and maybe a good Martini. Bill did his best to blend in but his disheveled appearance was a dead give away. He located a high table in the back, near a big bay window and set in at a vintage position to catch every nuance coming and going. He caught glimpse of himself and didn't recognize the reflection in the window. He caught sight of his growing receding hairline and chuckled, as he couldn't recall the last time he didn't sport a clean-shaven head.

He remembered the bet he lost some ten years ago at a sports bar in San Diego. The Chargers were an eight-point underdog to the Raiders but he sensed an upset in the making. Lisa, a staunch Raider fan suckered him into a bet he couldn't refuse. She wagered anything he wanted against her having the pleasure of shaving him clean, from head to toe. Having experienced her sexually in every which way possible before, she knew just where his mind would wander and he did not disappoint her. He pretended to ponder the bet and came up with what she already knew he's been lusting for. He ticked off all of their conquests: sex on Black Beach's infamous nude cliffs in the middle of a busy weekend, a threesome in the call room at the U Institute with her best friend, the Mile High Club on a trip to Cabo; the latter made him smirk as he stared intently into her eyes knowing she was equally recalling their tryst some 30k miles up in the air on their eventual trip to Dubai.

He seemingly thought long and hard, moaned, and slowly stroked his goatee as he pretended to suddenly arrive at an epiphany. "Yes!" he nodded to no one in particular.

He turned to her and proclaimed, "I'll gladly let you shave me if you win," he said, "but WHEN I win, I'll bring 'the butta' and fuck your sweet little ass hole till you cry uncle," was his fair and equitable wager. She playfully stiffened and considered his offer. She'd always turned him down before; his size had always intimidated her, as she could never muster up the courage to let him penetrate her that way. She mulled it over and finally accepted the challenge with a firm handshake, knowing full well that half of the Chargers' starting line up was still smarting from the thorough ass whooping they received from the Broncos the previous Thursday. There was no way she could lose she thought, but the specter of shaving him or getting summarily fucked excited her. It was a win-win proposition.

The game turned out to be a closely fought match but in the end, the Raiders prevailed by three points. Bill protested that they did not cover the spread but she successfully argued that the spread was indeed a factor but not clearly a part of the deal. Later that night and much to his chagrin, Bill found himself fully lathered in the bathtub, staring at the sharp end of a straight razor's edge. She relished the moment and took her time shaving him cleaner than a patient being prepped for surgery. Not a single drop of blood was lost. When done, she led him to the bed and lathered him with his favorite after-shave balm, Truefitt and Hill, that she'd introduced him to the Christmas prior. She was pleased that the bottle was half used. Boy was he hard to shop for; she giggled at the thought.

In the end, she was so turned on to finally have total control over Bill that they made love all night long and as an exclamation point, she gladly offered him her prize possession. To her surprise, she thoroughly enjoyed him taking her that way that she couldn't wait to try it again. And so began the sexual education of Lisa, a process that lasted his entire internship year until she discovered that she wasn't his only student at the U.

Several drinks later, Bill decided to order some food. He couldn't remember the last time he actually ate. From across the room, he took notice of the overly attentive waitress who took his order who was now engaged in a conversation with someone he surmised was the manager. They both gazed at the TV monitor and than back to him.

To Bill's surprise, his likeness was frozen on the TV screen with the caption of "WANTED" boldly scrolling beneath it. He then saw the picture of Chris, his cellmate followed by an apartment cordoned off with the recognizable yellow tapes and multiple squad cars with lights ablaze surrounding the scene. Confused, he continued to stare at the TV, missing the manager's phone call until he hung up the phone.

It didn't take a genius to surmise that something untoward has happened to Chris and that he was somehow allegedly involved with it. A multitude of combinations of events ran through his mind.

Bill did not like any of them, given the occurrences of the past few days. He slowly gathered his belongings and started for the front door until he noticed the black and whites and a Crown Vic haphazardly parked on the front lawn of the Elephant Bar.

He quickly withdrew to the back of the restaurant, to the bathroom.

"Wait! Stop!" came a loud burst from the manager who rushed in Bill's direction in an apparent effort to thwart his retreat.

Reflexively, Bill shoved him through the buffet table and fortunately no one saw his action but the loud crash of the manager through the assorted greens and dessert trays was heard by all. The salad bar was tossed about and the multitude of dressings flung upon the windows, light fixtures and everyone within reach. That was enough cover for Bill to make his way to the bathroom area. To his benefit, the employee's lounge was nearby and Bill was able to escape out the back door and into the parking lot without any more interferences. He quickly made his way to his nondescript Piece Of Shit rental car, entered it and again slouched behind the seat and waited.

Under the cover of darkness, he was able to hide and observe the uniforms fall through the back door, scanning the whole parking lot for him in the opposite direction.

They made a futile effort and soon thereafter, returned to the bar.

Bill started the car and slowly made his way out of the parking lot. Again, he passed Detective White and almost felt obliged to wave at her, but thought better of it.

He cruised down the boulevard and soon made it back to the interstate with no particular destination in mind.

# Chapter 16

Bill made his way down the 99 Freeway, intending on continuing down to San Diego all the while running through the events of the last few days in his head. Nothing still made sense.

His predicament was indeed dire at best. Thirty minutes south of Fresno, the CNN report about him blared through his satellite radio; he had indeed become a well-known wanted man and he may not make it to Southern California if he got pulled over so he slowed down his speed. He had to hide and his immediate destination was now apparent. The next exit to Visalia loomed in front of him and he realized he could easily hide in the Sequoias, a place he knew very well from his days as a Visiting Resident in Anesthesia.

He took the exit for Highway 198 and he soon breezed into Visalia, and too many memories flooded back in his mind. The almond trees not withstanding by the golf course were in full bloom and his allergies to them did not disappoint. His eyes itched and the sneezes followed and kept coming non-stop. "Now I remember why I left this shit ass town!" He frowned.

He wanted to continue past the town into the Sequoias, as far from the trees as he could get but the familiarity of the town got the best of him and he exited on Goshen Avenue. He continued north, found Country Club Lane and soon found himself at a habitual address he had not visited in 9 years and pulled into the driveway. He automatically killed the engine and leaned back into his seat; he inhaled deeply and let the air out ever so slowly. It's been a long time since he'd been here but he felt right at home. However with much trepidation, he got out of the car, lumbered to the door and rang the bell, realizing that it was well past visiting hours. Suddenly, Bill did not feel so sure of his choice of destination and thought about reversing his step but the door flung open before he quite made up his mind. Debbie, never at a lost for words, silently froze, confirming that he would be the last person on earth she expected to ring her doorbell.

After a few long and agonizing minutes, Bill managed a wry smile through his customary and smirky demeanor and asked, "Are you gonna invite me in or what?"

She still did not respond.

Bill moved towards her as if attempting to hug and kiss her and surprisingly with all her might she reflexively reared back and slapped him across the face; his eyeball jiggled. She liked that.

He smiled.

She gritted her teeth and powered up for a repeat performance but he literally beat her to the punch and grabbed her by the waist, pulled her forward and planted a full on kiss on her lips.

She feigned resistance but soon gave in and embraced him. She jumped up and wrapped her legs around him and held on as if her life depended on it. In no time, she began to sob as he slowly inched the two of them into the house. She finally let go, stepped back and took full inventory of him.

"I envisioned attending your funeral in the very near future Bill! All that crap on the TV! What the fuck have you been up to love?"

Her face betrayed the hurt she had, recalling how he had abandoned her, how she'd been plotting his execution for the pain and hurt he'd imparted on her, how she fucking hated him for that. None of that mattered anymore. "He's in front of me right now; I still love him," she thought.

They both fell silent.

"Are you Ok?" she finally asked. "I can't believe the things they are saying about you in the news. Please tell me they are not true Bill?"

He shook his head and vehemently denied all the stories but he also admitted that things didn't look good for him.

She made her way to the wet bar and Bill looked around, re-familiarizing himself with her place.

"Still a Vodka Martini drinker?" she inquired.

"Yes please," he replied. "Some things will never change love!" he added. She quivered at the sound of that, knowing full well that he was blowing smoke up her ass, not even sure if he actually remembered what her ass looked like; she grinned.

She was flattered nonetheless.

They drank and got up to speed on their respective lives. She surprised him with her ascension in the medical field. She was a scrub tech when they first met at the U in San Diego but now she headed the blood bank facility in town. Once upon a time, they were first in heat then in love with each other. She followed him here to Visalia and things were peachy until his infamous encounter with Kelly during his rotation in Fresno. He came home one day and informed her that they were done; he finally experienced what true love was like. He moved out shortly thereafter, although they maintained sexual contact until he graduated and married Kelly and moved to Fresno.

He cringed at that recollection.

It'd been so long ago that she smiled at the same thoughts. In hindsight, he actually did her a favor, given the sordid details of his private life that were being played out over the airwaves of Central California and the world.

Bill recounted all the details of the past few days to her; she was always a good listener, he remembered.

Debbie peppered him with a multitude of questions and it all came back to the same point. How could his blood from a simple cut be all over not one but two distinctly different crime scenes? To him the answer was simple: his blood was planted there. Why? How? And by whom?

They continued their chat about his predicament but soon found themselves reminiscing about their times at the U. He was single handedly responsible for her termination as a tech in the OR, but again, professionally speaking, he was the best thing that ever happened to her.

Soon after his arrival as an intern, Bill was smitten with Debbie but was hell-bent on keeping his professional demeanor and not fraternizing with the staff. At least that's what he was told on numerous occasions during his many lectures within the department; never eat where you shit, son. Or was it the other way around?

The point was that the staff was off limits and he was not about to be the first intern to violate that mantra. It didn't take long for Bill to find out that that rule they had drummed into him was pure bullshit and in fact, he was the only one holding to it; they were all fucking one another. The staff and doctors spent so much time together in the hospital that they were more familiar with each other than their respective families at home. The hospitals were responsible for more marriages and divorces than any other profession known to man.

It all started so innocently. On his first day at the hospital, he had trouble getting into the men's locker room so she stood aside and watched him from a vantage point. She finally approached him and allowed him to use her badge to unlock the door. He jokingly told her that he would never have pegged her for someone who knew how to access the men's locker room and she replied that he would be amazed at her skill level. "Ditto," he replied with a wink, she smiled as she retreated; "game on," they both thought.

Thereafter, she would openly flirt with him and he would pretend not to notice. She would bring him coffee, home baked goods, and leave little trinkets—usually golf related—on his anesthesia cart, all against rules and regs of the Operating Room. She would write 'good morning' and 'have a great day' notes on his anesthesia machine and all took notice. He would smirk each time and gently wipe them off of his screen before logging in for the day. The whole staff grew to accept that they were an item but no one spoke openly of it.

She would coyly recount to her colleagues her fictitious nights spent with him and how they made love till the break of dawn and he never corrected her. The truth was that he never even knew where she lived until much later but everyone swore that they had spent every night together. It was all fun and games at first until he faced the wrath of his Chief Resident who pined for Debbie but couldn't accept that he was much too nerdy for her liking.

Unfortunately for Bill, the Chief had concluded that he was the reason that she rebuked him and took it all out on him. Bill garnished the worst possible schedule and cases but Bill undauntedly rose to the occasion and excelled at every turn until the chief acquiesced and finally moved on.

Bill knew that he couldn't ignore Debbie much longer; she was relentless. He made a point to have someone in the room with him every time he was scheduled to work with her; Debbie didn't care. She shamelessly flirted with him until he made a deal with her. He would go out with her if she toned down the antics at work; they were definitely interfering with his professional pathway. They shook on it and made plans to take a road trip in Visalia, a town he was scheduled to interview in for his next rotation in Anesthesia. They even made a reservation at the Vintage Press, a popular restaurant in town. She gladly accepted the offer, knowing full well, someway somehow, that someone from the new hospital would spot them and the rest would be easy from there.

Much to her chagrin, Bill got called in to an emergency surgery and had to cancel the date 30 minutes prior to their scheduled departure time so the trip never happened; a familiar theme to come. He apologized profusely and promised to make it up to her. She admonished him that she will not be so agreeable a second time.

The flirtation continued at work since he had yet to deliver on their agreement.

One day, Bill was assigned to the neurosurgery room on a case scheduled to last over 10 hours and Debbie took full advantage of her captive prey. The neuro room was the only one set up with the anesthesia machine against the back wall, with absolutely no traffic behind it; no one could see beyond the curtain. She was well aware of that and plotted to have the upper hand with that set up. Two hours into the case, Debbie came in and proceeded to seduce him in ways he never expected. She walked in, chatted with the whole crew in the room and finally made her way behind the sterile curtain that separated Bill from the surgical case. Under normal circumstances, that would be innocent enough as the head of the table would be the best vintage point for any visitor to observe the actual procedure and she took full advantage of that. Debbie, a diminutive person of five foot one, brought a stepping stool and placed it at the head of the table and seductively took her time stepping on it and peered just over the curtain. She exaggerated her posture, tippy-toed and feigned interest in the case. She watched and asked a few questions and then turned around just in time to catch Bill eying her derriere. She smiled.

With the room arranged the way it was, they were both fully aware that there would be no one sneaking up behind them.

Unabashed, his eyes never moved off of its intended target. She raised the stakes by slowly wiggling her ass towards him and then, she slowly released the drawstring to her scrub bottom and gravity did the rest, exposing her firm and round butt framed by pink G-string panties inscribed with the word "Hi!" across the top. "Dammit to hell; another setup!"

Her dance continued. She didn't have to turn around to know that she had his undivided attention. He was transfixed by her audacity and had to top her move. He reached over and parted her cullote. That surprised her. She turned towards him. He held her gaze and with his other hand, he pulled down his facemask and smiled. He sucked and wetted his long finger and in one motion slid it deep inside her ass. She gasped causing the scrub tech involved in the case to drop an instrument on the floor, barely missing the patient's exposed cranium. The surgeon frowned and froze in place. Everyone, sensing that they were up to no good, turned and stared at the two of them in unison.

Debbie faked a sneeze, avoided making eye contact with any of the surgical team members and the procedure soon resumed. She looked back at Bill who pantomimed silence to her with one finger extended over his mouth as he slowly sucked on his finger and again repeated his earlier move. This time she stayed quiet but her body language expressed her full enjoyment.

Bill stood up and equally dropped his scrub pants, exposing his full erection through his undies. She reached back and took her time exploring its contents before she exposed then stroked his cock from stem to stern.

He reached over to his machine, opened the top draw, located a tube of lubricating jelly and squeezed out a liberal portion in her hand. She knew exactly what to do with it.

He contemplated his next move and his mind was more or less made up for him as she lightly tugged at his cock in her direction. He obliged, grabbed her by the waist with both hands and entered her with depth precision as he towered over her while faking interest in the surgical procedure in progress. She moaned softly but loud enough for the surgical team to hear and they again froze. They both giggled. Bill continued his rhythmic penetration of Debbie, enough for the OR table to begin to shake in unison to their rhythm. Dr. Briggs, pretty pissed by now, turned and stared at the two of them. Debbie's eyes were closed and even with the mask on you could make out her gaping mouth. There was no denying what was going on on the other side of the surgical drape. Dr. Briggs' face turned several shades of crimson as he reached and pulled the drape, exposing how close Bill was standing behind Debbie but fortunately their bare bottoms were well hidden by the OR table. Dr. Briggs threw the scalpel he was still holding against the wall, ripped off his gown and mask and stormed out of the room. The rest of the team simply remained frozen in place. By the time Dr. Briggs returned with Debbie's supervisor, the two of them had wrapped up their shenanigan and feigned innocence.

The smell of sex clearly in the room betrayed the two of them but no one spoke about the events that just transpired. Half the staff were great friends with Debbie and the other half feared Bill's standings with the hospital's Board of Trustees.

In the end, the only thing to come of the ensuing investigation was a reprimand of Dr. Briggs for tossing the scalpel against the wall. Debbie was quietly reassigned to the lab but thereafter became inseparable from Bill. There wasn't a place in the hospital that they weren't spotted having sex sometimes with multiple others. They both added tall tales to their legendary antics and before long, no one could distinguish fact from fiction. As graduation grew closer, it was of no surprise to anyone that he was not asked to stay on staff in spite of his great academic accomplishments.

Bill eventually relocated to Visalia and Debbie followed him soon thereafter.

After several rounds of Martinis and storytelling, Debbie excused herself and headed for a much needed bathroom break. When she returned, Bill was curled up on the sofa, fast asleep. She stared at him for a few and assumed that he needed some rest and left him alone; not much has changed, she thought. She retreated to her bedroom and returned with an assortment of blankets and covered him; he didn't stir. She located her laptop and retired to the back patio with a nagging thought in mind.

She logged in and did a quick search on blood evidence and analysis; there were not many relevant items there. She located and called an old colleague, Dr. Fukishima, and picked his brain on the subject matter.

If Bill was to be believed, the crime scenes were a definite setup and contaminated, but the two of them couldn't quite figure out why and how. After several ideas were floated back and forth, Dr. Fukishima suggested that she contact an old friend of his, Dr. Simmons who he recalled did a lot of radical studies on blood conservation some 20 years ago. She hung up and googled him and found a huge cache of articles. An hour into her reading, she located a piece about an unsolved murder that occurred in Seattle some years back. She put it aside sensing no real connection to what she was looking for until she read the next article, which seemed to implicate Dr. Simmons in a cover up. She quickly scanned it and got the gist of the story. Dr. Simmons, a well-known physician and researcher was accused of planting evidence at a crime scene that he worked on as the ME, Medical Examiner. The case centered on incriminatingly high levels of EDTA that was found at the crime scene. EDTA is a preservative that prevented blood from clotting; thus a collected sample could be analyzed as close to its natural state but with nefarious ideation, it could also be made to appear as fresh blood. Fortunately, as in this case, EDTA can be tested for if one is suspicious enough to test for it. In addition to the above, the suspect had an ironclad alibi during the time that the crime was allegedly committed.

Interesting, she thought. She reviewed a few of the earlier articles and got excited. She forged on this time narrowing her search for medical related murders. There were quite a few of them but none seemed to hit close to home.

Frustrated, she slammed the laptop shut and let out a few expletives. She returned inside, some while later, thought about waking Bill up and filling him in on the details that she'd learned; but truth be known, she wasn't ready to admit to herself that seducing him would have been her real motive for waking him up. She sheepishly let that thought go and decided that it all could keep till morning.

She grabbed and refilled her Martini glass and retired for the night, solo. In a tipsy and blurred vodka haze, she drifted off to sleep and woke up the next morning with the same thoughts from her session on the laptop from the night before.

She made her way back to the den and, true to form, Bill was still in the same position she had left him in; he barely stirred as she brewed a fresh pot of coffee. She grabbed a cup and her laptop, and retired to the patio to finish her search. She quickly arrived at the same conclusion as before and slammed the laptop shut, closed her eyes and let out a slow and deep breath.

"You know it's usually operator error and not the computer's fault if the results aren't satisfactory," said Bill from behind her. "Research is an interesting mistress; if you massage her just right, she will confess", he added.

She was so engrossed in her search that she never heard him step out onto the terrace, with a cup of coffee in hand. "He still remembered where I keep his favorite mug," she thought.

She paused for a moment and summoned him to her; he obliged. She filled him in on her findings but he was too distracted to make sense of it all until she stated that she was having trouble tracking down the so called expert in the field named Dr. Simmons; it was as if he fell off the map over the last five to eight years or so.

She offered to refill his mug but he opted for some water instead. She handed him the laptop and headed inside. He opened it to her last page then put it down on the chair, waiting for the page to boot up. Something caught his eyes when he returned to it and stared at a full headshot of Dr. Simmons.

"I know this man," he said out loud to no one in particular. "He's aged a bit but there is no mistaking who he is. Why would he change his name?"

Bill went through the articles with such voracity that he almost dropped the laptop on the floor. Debbie returned and he excitedly explained it all to her, at least what he could make of it. She concurred that he had to return and sort out this new detail.

"Should we call the police?" she asked.

He waved her off and had a multitude of excuses as to why he was not ready to collaborate with the police until he knew where this was going. She reluctantly agreed and she ushered him to the front door.

They exchanged their goodbyes and he promised to return for a longer visit, but right now, he had a one-track mind. He knew he had to go see the one person who could put this all together.

The only thing that remained to be answered was whether this person would be part of the problem or part of the solution.

Soon, Bill was back on the 99 Freeway North, heading back to Fresno. He picked up his phone and called the hospital to check in on Kelly. The news was no better than the last time he called. He hung up and contemplated calling Lexxi. Finding no real reasons not to, he mindlessly dialed her number and she picked up on the second ring; he liked that.

Her melodic accent paralyzed him once again as she sounded so happy to hear from him. Bill reminded himself that he'd been meaning to ask her about her exact background but each time the thought slipped his mind as he got lost in the canorous cadence of her voice.

All he remembered from their last conversation that night was that she's from one of the Caribbean Islands, but which one he was not sure. She immigrated to England with her mother at an early age to escape an abusive husband and father. Her mother remarried and ironically, she ended up in the exact same situation with her new husband, a Baptist minister from West Africa. Lexxi was raised in the very narrow strictness of the church and eventually left home at the ripe old age of 16 for New York to stay with relatives, in order to escape the glares and touches of her stepfather. Lexxi's body was starting to fill out and she noticed that her stepfather was starting to take special interest in her curves and that creeped her out. Her mother was of no help so she took matters into her own hands. Two years later, since that situation turned out to be no better than back home, Lexxi hit the road to Los Angeles to pursue a career in films and lord knows what else. She left with her best friend who was fairing much worse than she was at the hands of her biological father.

They had a great time traversing the country and eventually made their way to L.A. and that was where the fairytale story ended. She lost contact with her best friend and several waitressing jobs later, she ran into a nice guy who seemingly took interest in her. It didn't take long for that situation to turn abusive and she ended up on stage, dancing to anyone's fancy at the strip club. She serendipitously escaped that scene and ended up at her present gig at the hospital. But by then, Lexxi had grown accustomed to the finer things in life and a clerk at the hospital did not pay well enough for her taste. So, she returned to the only job at which she ever excelled. She'd been meaning to leave the club scene but the lure of the money had kept her fixated in place.

Bill and Lexxi exchanged pleasantries and he stayed on the line much longer than he intended to and his whereabouts were quickly triangulated on the cell towers by the FPD. They had him dead to right but Detective White gave strict orders that he was to be followed and not apprehended; she wanted to know what the good doctor was up to. He had a chance to flee but he chose to return. Her first thought was that he was heading to the hospital to finish off Kelly but his eventual route said differently. Bill was so engrossed in this latest development that he failed to pick up on the obvious tail he had on him since shortly after he left Visalia half an hour ago.

He made his way into North Fresno and located his destination; he'd been to that house before, most recently during last year's Christmas party, the last party he attended with Kelly.

Bill pulled into the parking space next to the black pickup truck he'd remembered seeing before at Lexxi's place; the hair on the back of his neck bristled. The answer he sought quickly changed from a solution to a definite problem. Little did he know, his every move was being recorded on the surveillance system recently installed by a paranoid doctor some while ago. He got out and went around the black truck, past the hedges, and past those hideous pink flamingos in the front yard and made his way to the front door. He rang the bell, but there was no answer so he rang again. By then, Detective White's and 2 other Crown Vics were strategically stationed down the road, in full view of the front door, waiting for the next move.

Bill grew impatient. He paced about the entryway and then reached for the doorknob, tried it and the door swung wide open.

He cautiously entered and was immediately struck across the back of his head with a blunt object and he fell the rest of the way in.

Without further prompting, all 3 Detectives hurriedly exited their cars and made their way to the house. The front door was once again locked by the time they tried it as Bill did; they cautiously proceeded to the rear entry and to their pleasant surprise, they found a wide-open sliding door. Fearing some kind of trap or a large animal, they guardedly entered one at a time and first cleared the den. Thereafter they fanned out and continued to clear each room in succession until they reached what appeared to be an office on the ground floor; they could barely make out the conversation on the other side of the door. They silently approached it and peaked in through a gaped door. They saw Bill, strapped to a chair; his head slumped down to his chest. He had an IV line taped in his right antecubital fossa, connected to a large dripping saline bag. Detective White heard the voice but did not immediately recognize the man standing behind Bill. She looked at the other two Detectives and pondered their next move; they concisely decided to wait it out. In the meantime, they observed the man reach in his pocket and slowly pull out a syringe, squirt out the air bubble and without hesitation inject half of its contents in the IV line. They thought about rushing in but Bill began to stir back to life, albeit still very groggy, so they decided to again wait it out and see how this would play out.

The man circled Bill and faced him with nothing but pure anger on his face. He proceeded to berate Bill for the asshole that he is. He struck Bill across the face with an opened palm, albeit in a less than a masculine way, and laughed out loud; it felt good.

"Hahahaha! I've been meaning to do this for a very long time!" he yelled closely at Bill's face. He reared back and struck him again. Bill moaned out loud, as consciousness returned to him. He stretched against the restraints but remained stuck in place. The rage within him began to well up. He stirred some more but couldn't free himself. That made him furious!

The assailant continued to recount the many times that Bill had belittled and humiliated him in in front of the staff, his colleagues, and patients alike.

"I'm a fucking better clinician that you could ever dream of becoming Dr. Presser! I've saved your ass on so many occasions and yet you continue to act as if I don't matter. Really dude? Instead, you assign me to all of your demeaning committees; the Well-FUCKING-Being Committee Bill? Are you kidding me? I petitioned for a seat on the Med Exec Committee thinking that I could make a difference as a leading physician in the community and you humiliated me by actively countering my campaign! YOU FUCKING HUMILIATED ME BILL!!!!!!! I tried to assume the high road and not take any of this personally but your antics continued. I truly wanted to know what exactly did I do to deserve this kind of treatment, Bill. I asked around and the best answer that I could get was that you were a class one, certifiable fucking asshole. A motherfucking asshole Bill! Did you know that? That's what everyone think of you Bill! Your latest transgression was the last straw. Hearing the giggles to your name-calling of my wife as she lay dying on the OR table still haunts me my friend. Calling her Fat Forty and Fertile was uncalled for. You have no idea how hard she dieted! Right then and there I knew that that you had to pay and pay dearly for that. You had to feel my pain! I haven't had this strong of an urge for revenge in long time Bill. You brought this monster out again. It's entirely your fault Bill! Now you must pay, asshole!"

"I know all about your bitchy wife and mistresses," he went on. "Who do you think read all of those tests you ordered over the years? I know about all the STD's, pregnancies and miscarriages, Bill! I chose to remain professional and keep my mouth shut but you! But you, you are evil, Dr. Presser! Pure fucking evil! I loathe the very ground you walk on you dick-head; I've watched you walk in every fucking morning as you touch your name plate in the parking lot as if it's your crowning glory of achievement. I'm here to tell you it's not; it's fucking not!!" He yelled as he struck Bill across the face again.

"You couldn't leave well enough alone. You had to come find me. I was content to watch you suffer without your perky little wife and mistress. Now I must destroy you just like I did all the others. No one must know that I am the former Dr. Simmons. I buried him long ago but his work will live on."

Bill's head began to clear and he tried to speak but was not coherent enough to make any sense. He managed to mumble 'Kelly' and Dr. Ryan let out a big belly laugh. "Of course it was me!" was the response. "I took pleasure in gutting that little prissy bitch of yours. Sorry about the kid, Bill; it truly was an unintended consequence."

Bill angrily tried to reach for him but he was strapped in tightly and he could not release his hands.

Dr. Ryan went on to describe how he intended to frame Bill for the attack on Kelly by planting his blood all over their room, the crime scene. Vicky was just the bonus plan; he hated her too.

"Now it's your turn Dr. Presser. No one will find the body after I'm done with you." With that, he calmly walked over to the table, reached inside and grabbed a large syringe filled with a white substance. He strolled back towards Bill in a slow and deliberate manner, located an injection port on the IV tubing and connected the syringe to it. He looked back at Bill, smiled and raised the syringe. He was about to empty it into the IV line, into Bill, when Detective Afoot stepped in and yelled, "Freeze asshole!"

Unfazed, Dr. Ryan looked up, held his gaze and slowly continued his hand motion. Left with no other choice, Detective Afoot fired two rounds into Dr. Ryan's forehead. He slumped to the floor, releasing the syringe, but not before injecting a few cc's of the substance into the IV line. Fortunately for Bill, it was not enough to have a lasting effect on him.

All three detectives rushed over and released Dr. Presser from his bindings. After the obligatory inquiries about his status, they summoned the compliment of ambulances, morgue, CSI team, and so on. Detective White was still puzzled on how they got there. Bill filled her in on his happenstance discovery. Dr. Simmons was apparently implicated in the framing of several doctors in the past. However, those cases remained unsolved because of solid alibis and the amount of preservative found in the blood at the crime scenes.

He added, "I'm sure you will also find several unsolved murder cases, similar to the attack on Kelly, in locations that Dr. Simmons, now Dr. Ryan, lived." What tipped the scale at Debbie's house earlier was the fact that Dr. Ryan, then Simmons was conducting research on a new form of blood preservative that would not only keep blood from coagulating but would also be undetectable by modern tests. The Ethics Committee at his then hospital found too many issues with the latter and nixed the project. Apparently he continued his research and must have perfected it; that would be the only logical conclusion since no EDTA was found at his house or any of the other crime scenes for that matter. The answer to that conclusion became clearer as the team fanned out and located a storage chamber full of un-coagulated blood vials all clearly labeled and in alphabetical order with names, dates and blood types.

Bill quickly located his vial that was nearly half empty. He recognized it as the sample that was taken in the lab the day that he resuscitated Mrs. Ryan in the OR and was stuck by the uncapped needle left on the anesthesia cart.

"How ironic," he thought. He remembered questioning himself at the time for the need of such a large blood sample and dismissed it; now he knew why. More often than not, the labs would always collect a larger than necessary sample to run a test. At the risk of needing to re-run the test for whatever reason, they would rather have an ample sample on hand, thus reducing the timeline for a re-analysis but just as important, they would rather not bother the patient with another trip to the hospital for a duplicate blood draw; that would reek of incompetence. Most places would immediately discard the samples once the tests were completed. Apparently for nefarious reasons, Dr. Ryan found a way to maintain these samples indefinitely.

In all, 2,349 well-preserved samples and counting were found; there was another storage area yet to be entered. So far, they were all collected and sent to the lab for analysis. They will be compared with all the cases handled by Dr. Simmons/Ryan over the past 14 years; there would be many, several including Death Penalty cases in which there may have been a few executions. This was a prosecutor's worst nightmare, having cases tainted by a crooked staff or expert witness. That would have to be sorted at a later time.

For now, all four crime scenes would be re-evaluated for contamination and compared with the sample of Bill's blood found today. Detective White was so confident that a match would be found that she allowed Bill to be taken away unescorted by ambulance to the hospital for observation; he offered no resistance. She was doing him a favor, as he would be that much closer to Kelly. On his way to the hospital, his phone rang; it was the ICU calling. He was informed that things weren't looking good for Kelly. She'd been in progressive renal failure over the past 48 hours since she came in and has not responded to dialysis. The sepsis was not amenable to any treatment they threw at her. Unfortunately, she went flat line about 30 minutes ago and CPR was in progress. They needed his permission to withdraw care and he flatly denied them.

"Do your damn jobs, goddammit!" he shouted. "I'll fucking be there in less than 5 minutes," he angrily said. "I'll pronounce her if I have to!" he added and disconnected the line.

Deep down, he wasn't as sure that he would ever get the chance to even do that.

The ambulance rumbled at breakneck speed and made it there in record time and pulled up to the receiving dock at the Emergency Room.

Bill jumped out of the rig and ran like a madman through the ER and took the back stairs to the ICU three at a time. He crashed though the entrance and the eerie silence told him all he needed to know; his heart sank. He slowed his-gait, his chest heaved, and he looked about for a sympathetic eye. No one gazed at him. He saw Brenda outside of Kelly's cubicle and slowly made his way to her. She looked toward him but quickly averted his eyes. Bill walked over to her, looked through the window just in time to see Nurse Betty reach up and turn off the cardiac monitor. He looked down at the bed and Kelly, motionless, was shrouded in an unassuming white body bag, ready for the morgue.

Brenda reached up and hugged him as they both wept openly.

He was ushered to the Nurses' Lounge where a small crowd present quickly vacated the room. He was a mess as the weight of the past few days befell upon him. He openly wept as he repeatedly apologized to no one in particular.

Kelly and Vicky were dead and there was no denying that it was his fault. His antics, his humiliating treatment of everyone in front of him, his words, his suppression of anyone who threatened him professionally all came flooding back. To what gain? He felt so small and defeated and for the first time in his life, Bill admitted to himself that he was a horrible excuse of a human being.

"How did I get here?" He pondered. "Mother would be so disappointed," he accepted as he began to wail even louder.

A small crowd gathered about him. A few sympathetic colleagues corralled him and offered some kind of comfort. Finally, the IV team arrived, placed a catheter in his arm. He was sedated and the light slowly dimmed. It took several orderlies to usher him onto a gurney but his brain remained online for a few minutes more, enough to take notice of all of the people helping him. They were the same crowd he'd pissed on so many times over the years.

"I must do better," he thought, as his consciousness faded to black.

# Epilogue

Bill was indeed exonerated of all charges as Dr. Ryan was found to have staged all of the killings. His truck was forensically placed at all of the crime scenes and incriminating surveillance videos from the parking lot and the ICU caught distinctively clear images of him entering both areas during the times Vicky and Mrs. Robinson were killed. The evidence was overwhelming, now that they knew what to look for. Apparently Dr. Simmons was quite the prolific serial killer in the Northwest in yesteryears. There were at least half a dozen unsolved medically technical killings in every town that he was in then they suddenly stopped as of eight years ago. Detective White surmised that Kelly was his first killing as Dr. Ryan since a doctor's wife was found hacked to death in Seattle; just about the time he changed his name. He had stopped, but the urge, never completely gone, was rekindled by Dr. Presser's antics. He then was finally pushed over the top into action by Bill's perceived slight of his wife during the OR code.

With all the new findings, they were able to match his DNA to the vomitus found in Kelly's abdominal cavity. Apparently he had lost his resolve as an accomplished serial killer and made lots of mistakes.

The black truck was forensically linked to all of the crime scenes and the FBI was hard at work; so far linking him to at least a dozen unsolved murders along the Northwest corridor. Other perps were convicted and serving as much as life or death sentences for crimes that the system now knew that they did not commit. Their only failings were to simply have crossed paths with Dr. Simmons at a random lab; at least four of them were already executed.

Dr. Simmons was involved in at least 2,500 cases in his tenure as a Medical Examiner in Seattle, Los Angeles, and of course Fresno County combined. It is surmised, judging by the number of half-empty blood vials recovered at his house, he could easily be implicated in the cover up in at least half of these cases. It would take a long time to unravel all of them but in the meantime, Bill was trying to make sense of his new life.

Vicky's body was picked up by her family and taken back to Louisiana for burial. Chris, the solitary perp, was left unclaimed until Bill felt guilty enough to have him cremated and given a descent disposal.

Kelly was given a monumental send off that was attended by most of the staff from the hospital. Bill was surprised to see Lexxi in the back of the crowd. Once dispersed, he made his way to her and they chatted freely. He made all kinds of promises to keep in touch but now was not the right time, even though he felt some kind of attraction to her. He'd learned an invaluable lesson, the hard way, on human relations that he'd never cared to even consider before. His boorish behaviors had to change and for once in his life he had to admit that sex was not the answer to all his pangs.

They hugged and parted ways until next time. Bill made his way to the last remaining town car, slipped in, and quietly closed his eyes.

"Where to Dr. Presser?" was the gentle query from the front seat. He opened his eyes and gazed into the prettiest set of blue eyes he'd seen since, well Kelly.

"Home," he somberly responded, and shortly thereafter added. "Got any plans tonight, love? I could use the company of a stranger, no strings attached of course."

"Well my boyfriend may object," she replied.

"What he doesn't know... We'll send him a conciliatory gift in the morning and I promise I won't tell him if you don't," he added.

She smiled and contemplated the offer and closed the partition between the two compartments, all the while holding his gaze.

He returned her smile and took her response to mean that he won't be alone tonight. Satisfied, he leaned back and closed his eyes.

CPSIA information can be obtained
at www.ICGtesting.com
Printed in the USA
LVOW10s2312311017
554531LV00009B/209/P